SHERLOCK HOLMES
AND THE
CABINET OF WONDERS

The Early Casebook of Sherlock Holmes

Book Eight

Linda Stratmann

SAPERE
BOOKS

SHERLOCK HOLMES
AND THE
CABINET OF WONDERS

Published by Sapere Books.

24 Trafalgar Road, Ilkley, LS29 8HH
United Kingdom

saperebooks.com

ISBN: 978-0-85495-557-2

Dedicated to the memory of Thomas William Tobin, chemist, architect, science lecturer, and innovative creator of optical stage illusions.

From
Memoirs of a Medical Man
by A. Stamford FRCS

1924

CHAPTER ONE

There is a popular saying, 'every one must believe his own eyes'. Whoever the originator of this ancient axiom might have been, he had not understood the quirks and peculiarities of our sense of vision. The eye is the master of deceit, and the fount of illusion. Ask any conjuror.

During the course of my long career in medicine, the mysteries of the eye were gradually being solved, but in 1878, the year in which I took my final examinations in surgery at St Bartholomew's Medical College, there was much that lay enticingly hidden. The structure of the eye was already well-understood through dissection. We knew how it received light from the external world and made images accessible to the brain. But we were also aware that in addition to the physical eye, there is the eye of the mind. It is the mind which, when functioning correctly, applies logic and judgement to the pictures it receives from the eyes, corrects errors of the senses, and alerts us to possible deceit. At least it is able to do so much of the time, but even for the keenest brain there are exceptions. Sometimes even the best of minds will lead us astray.

Sherlock Holmes, when others fail to perceive what he does, is often wont to say, 'You see, but you do not observe.' This is because his skills of analysis are of a higher order than most. He uses his advanced sense of logic to see beyond deceit.

In my student days I had already determined that ophthalmology would be my specialism when I acquired my own practice. I was therefore particularly eager to attend a lecture in which the class was to be presented with examples of illusions that deceive both eye and brain. The lecturer, while admitting to being merely an amateur dabbler in the art of legerdemain, was able to demonstrate sufficient facility to prove his point. We all knew that playing cards could not suddenly vanish and then instantly reappear. Nevertheless, by his skill, he fooled our eyes into informing us that this was what had happened. When making a coin seem to fly invisibly from under an inverted cup to another, the action of one hand to which he drew our attention so distracted us, that our minds were unable to gather that it was the other hand which had created the illusion. If we wanted further proof, he said, we should visit the Egyptian Hall in Piccadilly, a theatre famously known as 'England's Home of Mystery' where the French conjuror Monsieur Gaston, whose skill in sleight of hand was said to be second to none, was appearing under the auspices of the leaseholders and celebrated magicians, Maskelyne and Cooke.

I needed no urging, and as soon as the lecture had ended, I hurried to the box office to buy a ticket for that evening's performance. On a sudden impulse, I bought two.

It was late February, I recall, and the weather that month had been dull and gloomy, with frequent foggy days only enlivened by bouts of stormy rain. In some ways the mood of the weather reflected that of Sherlock Holmes. He sometimes plunged into a state of languor when nothing would arouse his interest or attention, occasionally enlivened only by railing against his own frustration. There were no mysteries to stimulate his questing mind, no challenges to face, nothing to induce him to take one of his bold essays into deadly danger. He was, I felt sure, still experiencing the despair of self-doubt that had enveloped him the previous winter following a collaboration with his brother Mycroft. I had been hoping that once the spring season bloomed, he would emerge from the doldrums with renewed energy.

He had not been entirely idle. I often called upon him in his solitary rooms in Montague Street, and sometimes found him arranging his collection of newspaper cuttings or studying maps and directories. I occasionally brought him some pastries baked by my mother, and once, a volume on chemistry I had found in an old bookshop. He did not say so, but I thought, or perhaps I merely hoped, that he was touched by the fact that he was valued and missed. I don't know if Mycroft visited him. I decided not to ask.

With two tickets to the Egyptian Hall in my pocket, I went to see Holmes. As usual, his small living room presented a vision of clutter and careless disorder, which he insisted was his own singular method of arrangement, not to be disturbed by any other hand. A solitary Persian slipper, the souvenir of a previous adventure, had been pressed into use as a tobacco pouch. The atmosphere was singed with the odour of re-smoked dottle.

I found him slumped in an armchair with a pipe and a newspaper. He was wrapped in the dressing gown he usually wore when at ease, and I saw with some sadness that he had not shaved recently, and his hair required the attention of a comb. Nevertheless, he was pleased to see me, and when I launched into a description of the lecture I had attended and the display of dexterity I had witnessed, he greeted my account with a faint smile. Holmes is only a few months my senior, but he sometimes treats my enthusiasms with the amused indulgence of a parent listening to the innocent babble of a child.

'I have decided to go and see Monsieur Gaston for myself,' I said. 'I have a ticket for tonight, at eight. In fact, I have two tickets.'

Holmes gave me one of those looks which said that he had seen through my obvious ploy but was willing to indulge my humour. This was not a discouragement, and I pressed on. 'I was wondering if you would be so kind as to accompany me. I would like to seek your opinion on the art by which the eye might be deceived. The programme ends at ten, and then,' I added hopefully, 'perhaps we could have a little supper somewhere.'

There was a long reflective silence, then very slowly and deliberately Holmes folded his newspaper and set it aside. His tobacco had by now burned down, but he did not replenish it. He knocked out the dottle onto a saucer, where it joined an accumulation of the day's smokes, and replaced the pipe on its rack. Then he passed the knuckles of one hand thoughtfully across his chin, before running his long fingers through his dishevelled hair to smooth it out.

And that was how the adventure began.

CHAPTER TWO

If you were to walk down Piccadilly today, you might pause at number 170 to view a handsome stone portico above which are inscribed the words 'Egyptian House'. You might wonder why this otherwise unimpressive building is so named. Sadly, it is the only tribute to the old Egyptian Hall which once stood on that spot.

In its heyday there was nothing quite like it in London. Other buildings might have boasted fashionable salons with decor inspired by the classic style of old Egypt, but only in Piccadilly, standing proudly between the usual shops and cafés, appeared the exterior elevation of an ancient temple. Here one could stand for a while to admire the strange angular geometry, and statues of deities guarding the door, before stepping between fluted pillars carved in the form of papyrus plants into the promise of the arcane.

The Egyptian Hall was initially a museum, its galleries displaying collections of art and antiquities, sometimes enhanced by the delivery of a scholarly lecture. Its principal glory was the large hall, opulent and dramatic, its ceiling dominated by an ornamental dome, where the gods of ancient Egypt would have felt suitably honoured. Over time, the building's atmosphere of mystery and the obscure transformed it into a place of entertainment, most notably conjuring and illusion.

Holmes's taste in the theatre has always leaned towards the refined air of the concert hall, where he could appreciate the artistry of the world's leading violinists. He would then attempt to emulate them by scraping away on his own violin which he insisted was a Stradivarius, although to my knowledge he never put that claim to the test. He would not have appreciated more generally popular amusements, such as the broad humour of a pantomime. The performances offered by the Egyptian Hall were, however, said to be suitable for all ages, and careful never to offend good taste.

Once Holmes had agreed to accompany me on that dull February day, I was able to wheedle some hot water from his landlady, and he disappeared into his bedroom, emerging soon afterwards by some transformative magic washed, dressed, shaved, and groomed.

I already had a leaflet listing that evening's programme, which included dancing Chinese plates, legerdemain, a comedic presentation in which Mr Maskelyne would decapitate his associate Mr Cooke, an 'anti-spiritual séance' exposing the trickery of mediums, a human serpent, the Indian basket trick, and a game of whist featuring Maskelyne's famous automaton, Psycho. It soon became apparent to me that at least one item on this bill of fare had lit the flame of interest in my friend, but I decided not to enquire and let the fire take hold unassisted.

In view of the inclement weather, we took a hansom. Once we were settled in the cab, I tried to draw Holmes into conversation about the prospect of rain, and the crowded streets, and my anticipation of what the evening would bring. His responses were wordless. I hoped for better when we arrived at Piccadilly.

There was a busy flow of traffic outside the hall, and a jostling cluster of persons waiting for the auditorium to open. The Maskelyne and Cooke show was the subject of several large advertising posters, whose bold lettering was impossible for the passer-by to miss, even from across the road. A more conventional style of entertainment was also being promoted as taking place in the smaller hall upstairs, where Mr Jonathan Goodgold and his wife were performing a programme of comic sketches, music, dramatic recitations, and ventriloquism.

A new poster had just been affixed announcing next month's attraction in the small exhibition gallery. The 'Scottish Giant', William Campbell, the largest man in Britain, if not the world, reputed to weigh fifty-two stones, would be holding a series of levées where he would be presented to the public. I am not sure I like the practice of displaying living persons of unusual bodily proportions as novelties to be stared at, but from a physician's point of view I thought I might be able to learn from him if he was permitted to converse with visitors.

Holmes remained as stonily silent as a monument, but he gave his unaccustomed surroundings the gravest attention.

We made our way to our seats. The hall was rather smaller than I had anticipated, and I was reminded that it had only recently been converted for theatrical presentations, a purpose for which it had never been built. The atmosphere was both brilliant and intimate, with mirrors and chandeliers providing a reflective sparkle to the luxury of crimson draperies and the rich colour and comfort of new upholstery. A respectably dressed audience filled the auditorium, their murmured conversations suggesting pleasurable expectation.

When the curtains parted to reveal a modestly sized stage, I saw a table piled with decorative dinner plates, dessert dishes, and a few considerably larger vessels, which we had been promised would be made to dance for our amusement. It was the structure at the back of the stage that attracted my attention, the cabinet employed by Maskelyne in his exposure of séances. It most closely resembled a large wardrobe, crowned by a decorative carving. There were three doors, the centre one being provided with a small square aperture at head height while the two side doors were fastened with external bolts. It stood upon a low trestle so there was a clear space of several inches between the base of the cabinet and the floor.

The audience's mutterings became a burst of applause as John Nevil Maskelyne took the stage. He was then thirty-eight years of age, his thick black hair combed dramatically straight back from a deep pale forehead, and he sported a luxuriant dark moustache. Formally dressed in the manner of a conductor of music, he carried with him an air of generous bonhomie, the smile in his eyes suggesting that he was about to show us marvels.

Great as my anticipation was, it would have been still greater had I then known that when Sherlock Holmes next visited the Egyptian Hall it was to investigate a possible case of murder, and everyone who took to the stage that night would be a suspect.

CHAPTER THREE

It would take a whole volume to describe in detail the wonders I saw on that visit to the Egyptian Hall. I offer only my first impressions, not wishing to trouble my readers with the analyses and controversies published later by others.

Inevitably, in the domain of Mr Maskelyne and his associate Mr Cooke, their performances dominated most of the evening. Maskelyne's plate spinning, which he carried out with an expression of mischievous delight, was merely an opener, a tasty hors d'oeuvre to the heartier fare that was to follow. It was also a demonstration of the most breathtaking manual dexterity I had ever witnessed, after which we could not doubt that here was a master of his craft.

The next act on stage was Prince Chandra the Indian mystic, in silken robes and a bejewelled turban. He was accompanied by Princess Yasmin; a fetching young lady clad in layers of colourful and nearly diaphanous material. Prince Chandra was able to create some beautiful illusions, making gorgeous fabric flow from a brass vessel in such abundance it almost covered the stage, before regaling us with the famous Indian basket trick. Employing the mesmeric movements of a magic wand to induce Princess Yasmin to lie down in a long wicker basket, Prince Chandra closed and sealed the lid, trapping her inside. He drew a long shining sword, which he demonstrated was sharp by holding up a sheet of paper and slicing it into strips. He then thrust the sword repeatedly into the receptacle, eliciting screams from the interior, and gasps of horror from the audience. To impress upon us what had just occurred, he held up the sword to show bright red blood dripping from the point. Throwing back the lid of the basket he revealed that it was empty, and to our relief, the lady reappeared at the back of the auditorium, alive and uninjured, gliding cheerfully to the stage, waving to the audience as she went.

Mr Maskelyne, now enveloped in voluminous robes, returned to the stage in the guise of a quack doctor. He proceeded to persuade his patient — Mr Cooke in the garb of a country yokel — that he could cure headaches by removing the head. It was impossible to argue with his assertion that a headless man would not suffer any pain, and the patient was thereby induced to agree. Once the deed was done, however, the doctor proceeded to pick the pockets of his victim, and ran from the stage, pursued by the irate patient, with his head tucked under his arm. What might have been shocking if done differently was performed so amusingly that the audience laughed at the ridiculous sight.

Monsieur Gaston, the conjuror, next took the stage. He was a slender fellow with a Gallic moustache and an engaging smile with which he particularly favoured the ladies. His feats of legerdemain with cards, coins, hoops and billiard balls, had me considering which was faster — the movement of the hand or the eye, and wondering how science might find the answer.

'And now,' said Maskelyne, once again the great conductor, as he returned to command our attention, 'by popular acclaim, we perform our anti-spiritual séance, in which we show that those persons who claim to be mediums performing wonders through their connection to the spirits, are actually conjurers who conceal their trickery with shadows and darkness. I present the cabinet, within which the supposed mysteries of spiritualism are manufactured. This is a copy of the secret chamber of the once-famous Davenport brothers, who made their fortune by deceit, and despite frequent exposure, still have many believers. Tonight, you will see all. If anyone wishes to examine the cabinet, before I begin, then please kindly join me on the stage.'

I expected Holmes to accept the invitation, but to my surprise, he did not move from his seat. 'Are you not going to take a look?' I asked him.

'When a conjurer allows you such freedom, there is nothing to be learned from it,' he said, and resolutely stayed in place.

Several gentlemen in the audience responded to the offer. Mr Cooke, who was now dressed in his usual attire, and with his head affixed to his shoulders, came to conduct the volunteers up the steps onto the stage. Meanwhile, Maskelyne unbolted the two side doors of the cabinet and threw them open. The central door was bolted from within, and he reached in and opened this too.

I was surprised to see how simple the interior of the wondrous cabinet was: a single undivided compartment, its surface bare and unvarnished. A plank seat was fastened to the wall on either side, positioned so that two sitters would face each other, and on each seat lay a coil of rope. In the central portion was a shelf on which stood an assortment of hand bells, while a tambourine, cornet and violin rested against the back wall.

'You will observe,' said Maskelyne, 'that a man seated either to the right or the left, and securely tied with his hands behind his back, the ropes then passed through holes in the body of the cabinet and the seat, so he is unable to move from that position, and with his ankles similarly tied, will be unable to leave the seat or touch, let alone play, the musical instruments.'

Those audience members who had mounted the stage, having rapped firmly on both the exterior and interior of the cabinet, proceeded to knock on the doors, examine the bolts, and handle the ropes and the musical instruments. Some gentlemen knelt on the stage and passed their walking canes between the cabinet floor and the boards. Others mounted a stepladder provided by Mr Cooke, to examine the roof. Eventually all declared themselves content that everything was as it appeared to be, and there were no secret doors or windows, or places where an accomplice might hide.

Maskelyne and Cooke then entered the cabinet, each taking a plank seat, and sat facing each other, putting their hands behind their backs. The volunteers, one of whom was a seafaring man, who declared himself to be thoroughly expert with knots, were requested to use the ropes provided to tie the two conjurors securely into place, so they were unable to move or use their hands or feet. This, as evidenced by the effort on the faces of the volunteers, was done with fierce determination, as they strained to make sure the knots were tied as tightly as possible.

After this, as instructed by Maskelyne, the two side doors were closed and bolted, and by dint of passing an arm through the aperture in the central door, the interior bolt was also fastened. The gentlemen withdrew to the side of the stage, and the house lights were dimmed.

Hardly any time at all had passed before the clamour began. Bells rang, tambourines rattled, and the cornet played a merry tune, while flickering ghostly lights appeared. We saw hands waving at the small window, then the central door suddenly flew open, and the violin was pitched out onto the stage. Soon, all was still. The house lights went up, and the volunteers unbolted the side doors. Inside the cabinet, the bells, tambourine and cornet were placed precisely as they had been at the start, and Maskelyne and Cooke were still firmly tied in place.

'And now,' said Maskelyne, 'we will repeat the performance, only this time the doors will be open, and the lights will remain on. Gentlemen, kindly check to see that all is secure before we begin.'

The volunteers examined the knots and declared themselves satisfied before they again retired to the side of the stage. Holmes leaned forward with interest, his chin resting on one fist, and I recalled his fascination with the subject of knots, which he had told me were characteristic of certain occupations. The two prisoners soon demonstrated that no sailor's knot could hold a skilled conjuror. They were free in an instant, by what means I could not devise, since all I saw was a simple movement of the shoulders. They then repeated the musical entertainment, Mr Maskelyne showing himself to be quite a virtuoso on the cornet, before assuming the starting position and restoring all to where it had been.

As the audience applauded so Maskelyne emerged from the cabinet and took a bow. The cabinet, despite its substantial size, was then made to float into the air, carrying with it a smiling and waving Mr Cooke.

'I have a word of warning to so-called mediums,' said Maskelyne as the cabinet gently descended. 'If you defraud the public, beware. You might find your trickery laid open to all here on this very stage.'

While we considered this threat, we were entertained by Yamadaya the human serpent in the form of a black mamba; a marvellously supple and epicene figure, who performed sinuous exercises to music resembling the wailing tones of a snake charmer's pipe.

Maskelyne then reappeared to introduce his famous automaton, Psycho. This remarkable construction was carried onto the stage in several pieces which were assembled in front of our eyes. I suppose I had been expecting something like the chess-playing Turk which, in bygone times, had so astounded all who had seen it. I had never witnessed the Turk, but illustrations showed a figure seated behind a large wooden chest on which the chessboard rested. This chest was supposed to hold only clockwork machinery, but, as some cynical persons had pointed out, it was also large enough to conceal a chess master who could operate the figure's movements.

Psycho, however, was no such thing. A tiny figure tricked out like an Eastern mystic, less than two feet in height, it sat cross-legged on a box far too small to contain a living person. This in turn rested on the end of a clear glass cylinder. The whole apparatus was placed on a low wooden platform. No man's hand could have controlled its actions, no cords or wires could have made it move, no creature could have been concealed inside it, unless one could have trained a puppy to play whist. Psycho, as became clear, was no mere mechanical toy wound by a key to perform a series of preordained movements. Not only did it play cards with some gentlemen volunteers, and win, it could divine a number supplied by a member of the audience, answer questions by ringing a bell, and perform arithmetic.

My greatest pleasure that evening however, in the midst of all these wonders, was to see the brightness of my friend's eyes, the sure sign that his interest had been impelled into action. We talked over our supper that night with energy and animation. Holmes the bored idler was gone, the master detective had returned, and it would not be long before his skills would be urgently required.

CHAPTER FOUR

The rekindling of Holmes's interest in his work had some unexpected and occasionally amusing moments. He plunged forthwith into a detailed study of knots. His intention was to compose a monograph on the subject of identifying the occupation of persons simply by examining the knots they had tied. He also undertook some investigations in the dissection room at Barts into the kinds of impressions left on the skin by different kinds of ropes and cords. Holmes's already crowded rooms became a laboratory for his new study. The small space he had available for dining was suddenly bereft of dishes and cups, and filled instead with samples of rope, cord and twine, accompanied by extensive notes on their characteristics.

I was often invited to tie him by the wrists and ankles to see if it was possible for him to extricate himself, which with some practice he invariably did, becoming over time extraordinarily proficient. Even certain knots which were reputed to be impossible to escape, could be overcome if the victim was alert to the danger, and prepared himself by careful positioning of hands and fingers. The captor might therefore imagine his prisoner to be secure, when he was in fact still able to wriggle free.

I was only pleased that Holmes's landlady was incurious about his activities, for if she had peered into the room unannounced while we experimented with knot tying, she might have been tempted to call the police.

One evening, having partaken of a light supper and a glass of beer, Holmes began to talk about some of the mysteries he had solved before we met. I already knew of one from his college days, his elegant solution to the fate of the missing cummerbund, but on that occasion, he described at length the solving of the *Gloria Scott* mystery and the suggestion made to him by an astonished Mr Vincent that he should become a detective by profession.

'I had never before given it serious consideration, but at that moment my future became clear to me,' he said. 'Naturally, I began to assemble in my mind a list of those areas of knowledge and skills I needed to acquire, and it became obvious that no college anywhere in the world would provide such a varied range of courses. I had completed my second year at university and did not return. That was when I came to London and applied to Barts to study anatomy and chemistry. I maintained my bodily fitness by continuing my practice of boxing and the sword, which I had commenced at college, while my long walks familiarised me with both the broad and narrow ways of London. You will have observed that my reading has been wide and apparently without any definite direction. Of course, it does have one very singular direction, to equip me with the knowledge I require of human frailty and wickedness in all its forms. In the last few years, I have established a number of connections both professional and in society, which will be of great value.'

He paused, and in a moment of unusual distraction, reached for his pipe, then quickly withdrew his hand out of deference to me.

'There was one lesson I needed to learn,' he continued, 'and I have now learned it. How to deal with adversity and defeat. It has been the hardest one of all, but without it, I cannot advance. I am pleased to say that I have recently been able to advise Sergeant Lestrade of Scotland Yard on an apparently insoluble difficulty, and he applied my advice with notable success. We may see him make Inspector yet.'

In future years Holmes often displayed an arrogance about his abilities and triumphs, although he was able to admit his failures, which were few. Some might have found this confidence annoying, but he was only able to achieve it through many hours of diligent work, both mental and physical, and also because he had descended to the depths and returned.

One morning, some three weeks after our visit to the Egyptian Hall, I had barely finished my breakfast when Holmes came to my door demanding I accompany him at once. 'Where to?' I asked. I was, of course, occupied with my studies, but judging by Holmes's tone, I sensed that I was not being offered the option of refusing him.

'The Egyptian Hall,' he said, 'in the company of Lestrade. He is waiting for us.'

I rose from my chair, took my coat and followed Holmes without another word.

'It might be something, it might be nothing,' said Lestrade, as we joined him in the carriage that was standing outside, 'but in view of the work Mr Holmes has been carrying out recently, I wanted his eye on the mystery, informally, of course, before we release the body and put it down to accident.'

'Not Mr Maskelyne, I hope?' I exclaimed.

'No, one of the stage assistants,' said Lestrade, consulting his notebook. 'Thomas Tapper. Age about sixty. With Maskelyne and his company for five years. His landlady noticed this morning that he had not come home to his lodgings last night and was worried as he had recently been unwell. She sent her husband to the theatre to see if Tapper had been ill or had an accident. Maskelyne is usually on the premises from six o'clock.

'They found Tapper dead on stage in the mystery cabinet. The one where they do the séances. It looked as though he was trying to emulate Mr Maskelyne by tying himself up, and then found he couldn't escape. No-one saw him do it, and we think he was alone at the time. My theory is that he panicked, and it was too much for either his heart or lungs or both. But a doctor is on his way to confirm that. I just wanted an expert opinion on the knot tying before we release the body by cutting the ropes.'

'And Mr Maskelyne noticed nothing out of the ordinary when he arrived?' I asked.

'No, he would have gone straight to his workshop. He has been building some new mechanical marvel to amuse us. Apparently, it plays the cornet.' Lestrade glanced at Holmes as if my friend might have some questions or observations, but Holmes was silent. He was not about to say a word about the case until he had seen the body in its unusual situation.

A constable admitted us to the building, and we passed the shuttered box office and proceeded to the great hall. Any place where crowds usually gather can feel strange when empty, and a theatre especially so, as one so rarely experiences its special kind of quiet. I thought it no wonder that so many theatres claim to be haunted, as they are full of memories which make a powerful impression on the mind. I could almost sense the echoes of drama, astonishment and laughter.

There were a number of figures on the stage, and we mounted the steps to join them. Lestrade introduced us to Mr Maskelyne, whose customary air of bonhomie was attenuated by concern and sorrow. He introduced the surgeon, Mr

Eastley, a gentleman in his thirties, who was making notes of his findings. Tapper's landlord, Mr Fergus, a stocky fellow of about forty, was a carpenter who did occasional work for the Egyptian Hall and had let a room to the deceased man, whom he had known for five years.

All three doors of the cabinet were open to view, and the body of Mr Tapper, still tied in place, was seated to the right of the interior, bent at the waist, head forward, his chin resting on his chest. It was too dark inside to see his features and I noted only a tangle of grey hair.

'I have not yet moved the body, as requested,' said Eastley, 'but I anticipate that a post-mortem examination will show that he died from a failure of the heart due to fright, and the cooling of the body suggests that this occurred late last night.'

'He had been complaining of pains in the chest which he put down to indigestion,' said Fergus. 'I told him to go and see a doctor, but he kept putting it off.'

Maskelyne nodded. 'I had also observed that he was unwell, and when I told him to go home and rest, he declined, saying it was something he had eaten which disagreed with him.'

'Were the doors found in this position?' asked Holmes.

'No, the left and centre doors were closed,' said Maskelyne. 'During a performance, once Mr Cooke and myself are secured, the side doors are bolted from the outside, then the middle door is bolted from the inside, by an assistant or one of the volunteers putting his hand through the small opening. Mr Tapper was very familiar with that arrangement. The cabinet can be taken apart for transport when we tour, and he often did so and then assembled it again. After the performance the interior is made tidy, and all doors are closed and bolted. This morning, after being alerted that Mr Tapper had not come home, I made a search together with Mr Fergus to see if he was still on the premises. When I saw that the cabinet door to the right was unbolted, and slightly ajar, it suggested that someone was inside.'

'And you were here from six o'clock in the morning?' queried Holmes.

'I was. I always arrive early so I can work undisturbed. The front door was then locked. I admitted the charwoman who comes to clean the public spaces, but she had left before Mr Fergus arrived.'

'Do you recall the time of Mr Fergus's arrival?'

'Not precisely, but the street door was unlocked by then, since Mr Jennings had arrived to open the box office; he is usually here at nine o'clock, and he spoke to me. Naturally, once we found the body, the hall had to be closed to the public.'

Before we examined the body of Mr Tapper, Holmes embarked on a thorough and minute study of the cabinet. Seen from close up, it was not as stoutly made as it appeared from a distance. The whole structure, including the plank seats and shelf, was simply constructed from lightweight boards, the sections bolted together for easy disassembly. The ornamental carving above the doors cleverly concealed the attachments for the wires which would produce the levitation. Two holes had been drilled through both the side walls, just behind the seats, to enable the binding ropes to be threaded through, and there were similar holes in the seats. None of the musical instruments appeared to have been disturbed.

Maskelyne was entirely content to allow our close inspection. I recalled Holmes's comment that when a conjuror freely allows others to examine items used in his performance it means that we would discover nothing concerning his professional secrets. This led me to the thought that in the

Egyptian Hall we were in the company of those whose very profession was deceit.

Although the house lights were on, the interior of the cabinet was far too dim to allow the kind of close inspection Holmes intended to make. 'I shall require some more light,' he said. 'If you would permit me?' He reached into a pocket and produced a compact lantern. It was a device which, when hung on the chest from a coat button, allowed gentlemen to read their newspapers in unlit carriages at night, and it was also used by the more adventurous when exploring tunnels. In Holmes's profession he employed it to illuminate those clues which others had missed.

'Let me see it,' said Maskelyne. 'You will, I am sure, understand that I do not as a rule allow naked flames on stage, but I appreciate that today the special circumstances might demand it.'

Holmes offered the lantern for examination, and Maskelyne, after making a careful inspection, agreed that because of its pierced metal cover it was as safe as any enclosed candle holder. Holmes lit the candle, closed the cover, then squeezed his long limbs into the cabinet, where he faced the figure on the right-hand seat. I followed him, and together we made an examination of the deceased and the ropes that bound Tapper, as far as we were able to manage without disturbing the position of the corpse.

Mr Tapper's body was collapsed in the centre of the seat, his arms fastened behind his back, still held by the binding rope. His skin was cold to the touch and when I crouched down to see his face, I noted that his features were calm. Whatever fright he had suffered, the relaxation of the muscles following his death had erased any clue as to his dying emotions. He was clad in the working clothes appropriate to his occupation, shirtsleeves rolled back to his elbows, and his hands showed the marks and stains one would expect to see on someone who handled scenery and did carpentry and painting. Even when a man is no longer breathing there can be an odour of drink recently taken about the body, but I detected nothing. There was no external sign of any injury, and nothing we saw gave us a clue as to the cause of his death. That information could only be provided under the scalpel.

The two ends of the rope that bound Tapper had been threaded through the holes in the side wall of the cabinet, to encircle his wrists. Once securely knotted the free ends had been passed around his waist, where they were again knotted and brought around his back. They were then passed down through the holes in the seat, to tie his ankles together, and secure his legs.

Holmes used his glass to study every knot, and also the wear on the holes in the cabinet. As he did so, I saw a frown appear on his brow. I wondered what he had seen, but did not interrupt his work. He next examined the coil of rope that lay on the left-hand seat and compared it with the one that bound the corpse.

'Identical,' he said. 'Manila, I believe, strong and smooth.' He emerged from the cabinet and turned to address Maskelyne. 'I have seen your dark and light séance performance. Both you and Mr Cooke were then tied securely into the cabinet. Am I correct that these are the ropes normally employed?'

'Yes, they are the very same ones.'

'One would expect a certain amount of wear on the interior of these holes, from the threading of the ropes and any subsequent movement, which I can see, but in the case of the right-hand one, where Mr Tapper's body is secured, there are significant abrasions which look fresh, where the material has bitten into the wood. This is in keeping with the efforts he made to free himself. Do you consider that he would have been able to tie himself in this fashion?'

'Yes, I do,' said Maskelyne, 'especially as he had many opportunities of witnessing how it was done. Mr Cooke and I are able to free ourselves from our bonds no matter how they are tied by expert volunteers from the audience, and then after we have made free with the instruments, we can slip into the bonds again, giving every appearance of them having been tied all the time. That was how the Davenport brothers made their name, only they did not discourage the belief of their admirers that the effects were produced by spirits.'

'So, once Mr Tapper was tied, you believe he could have escaped without a struggle?'

'I understand your meaning,' said Maskelyne. 'Had he been in full health and strength, yes, I think he might have done so, easily. He often claimed that he was able to do so, although I have never seen it. But if he had been taken ill it might have been another matter. Perhaps his attempts to free himself failed and in his panic he struggled and tightened the bonds.'

'Have you examined these knots?'

'I have.'

'Do you think they were tied by an expert or an amateur?'

'Not by an expert,' said Maskelyne confidently. 'I am quite certain of that. When we perform, should there be a sailor in the audience he will often volunteer to tie us, but we are familiar with their skills. These are not sailors' knots.'

Holmes nodded. 'And since you regularly invite volunteers to carry out the tying, there are numerous persons who do not work in the theatre, who would have known how it was done?'

'That is so. The tying only, but not the escape or how we restore the position.'

'May I release the body now?' asked Eastley.

'By all means,' said Holmes. 'But once that is done, I wish to make a further examination.'

Eastley produced a penknife and carefully cut the ropes so they could be removed without disturbing the knots, then I assisted him in lifting the body from the cabinet and laying it on the stage. The advanced rigor mortis meant that the corpse could not lie flat, but retained its inflexible seated position.

Holmes then knelt over the corpse, still using the lamp and his glass. He paid especially close attention to the marks of the binding on Tapper's wrists. He then re-entered the cabinet and examined the location where Tapper had been seated. An exclamation signalled that he had made a discovery. He called for my assistance, and I joined him to hold the lamp, directing it as he instructed, into the interior of the holes through which the rope had passed.

Holmes took a pair of forceps and an envelope from his pocket, and extracted with great care, something he found clinging to the rough exposed wood inside the hole — something so small and delicate that it was almost invisible — and placed it in the envelope.

'What have you found?' I asked.

'Some threads rubbed from a rope,' he said. 'Significantly, they are darker and less smooth than the material of those tying Mr Tapper. Mr Maskelyne, do you use any ropes other than the ones found on Mr Tapper?'

'I do not. That was how the Davenports were exposed, when they were tied by ropes brought by volunteers which they could not easily escape. Since my performance is an exposure of fraud, the volunteers have no reason to test me.'

'I shall examine these fibres under the microscope and may be able to identify the kind of rope used,' said Holmes. 'But I feel sure that when Tapper died, he was tied not with the manila, but with this other rope. The marks on his wrists suggest something thinner and coarser, with a different interval in the ply. They do not match the thicker rope. The abrasions on the holes in the cabinet strongly suggest a struggle. He was tied in such a way that he was unable to free himself as he expected to do. The manila rope normally used has a smoothness which, if I am not mistaken, assists the escape, and may even be essential to its performance.'

Maskelyne said nothing but smiled and made a slight bow of acknowledgement.

'Mr Tapper may well have died precisely as Mr Eastley has suggested,' Holmes continued, 'but I believe that another person was present, a person who performed the initial tying with the rougher rope, and on Tapper's death, removed it, and replaced it with the usual one to make it appear that Tapper had tied himself as an experiment.'

'It seems highly improbable that his death was intentional,' said Maskelyne. 'It is not a method which ensures success.'

'Whoever tied him did not mean him well,' said Holmes. 'Did they mean to kill him? I reserve my opinion. Another factor may emerge at post-mortem. Were they careless of what harm was caused to him? Undoubtedly.'

Eastley arranged to have the body taken to the police mortuary, and Holmes requested and was provided with a sample of the manila rope used by Maskelyne.

'I'd better tell the wife,' said Fergus, who appeared relieved that the corpse was not to lie at his home until the funeral.

'Does Mr Tapper have any family to bury him?' asked Maskelyne.

'None that I know of,' replied Fergus.

'Very well, I will see to the funeral costs,' said Maskelyne.

'If you don't mind, sir,' said Lestrade, with a serious expression, 'we need to have a talk.'

CHAPTER FIVE

Before Mr Fergus left, Lestrade took his address, advising him that he should expect to be interviewed as a part of the police enquiry. Anticipating that the landlord would be seeking to relet the room without delay, Lestrade, with a stern look, warned him to touch nothing. All Tapper's personal property was to be carefully preserved for examination in case there was anything that might offer some useful information concerning his death. The sergeant then said he wished to interview Mr Maskelyne in private before making his report to the divisional station, and requested the presence of Holmes and myself in our capacity as special advisors to the police.

I was, rather fancifully, hoping we would retire to the magician's secret workshop as the most private location in the hall, but this option was not offered to us. Maskelyne suggested we use the small upper gallery, where we could be comfortably seated. This was the room where William Campbell, the Scottish Giant, was now holding court in the afternoons, and a capacious settle had been placed ready for him, with two rows of easy chairs for his admirers. The walls were hung with an exhibition of watercolours which I felt sure would fade into obscurity once the giant occupied the room.

Lestrade moved one chair about so that it faced the others and indicated that he wished Mr Maskelyne to sit there, an instruction which the noted conjuror accepted with good grace. Holmes and I were directed to sit on the front row beside the sergeant.

'Now then, Mr Maskelyne,' said Lestrade, opening his notebook, 'when did you last see Mr Tapper alive?'

'That would have been last night at ten o'clock, when the evening performance ended. Once the curtains are drawn, he comes on stage to see to anything that needs to be cleaned or tidied away. I went to my workshop, where I remained until I left the hall at about a quarter to eleven.'

'Was anyone else still there when you left?'

'As far as I was aware there was no-one in the building at that time. It is Mr Tapper's duty to check the premises to ensure it is clear before he leaves. The box office was already closed up, and all the other performers would have gone home.'

'What time does Tapper usually depart?'

'Once his duties are done, no later than half past ten. This gives him time to visit a hostelry where he likes to go for refreshment before he returns to his lodgings — the King George Tavern.'

'Did you hear anything suspicious between ten o'clock and your departure?' asked Lestrade, scribbling in his notebook.

Maskelyne allowed himself a slight smile. 'No, Sergeant. I am currently perfecting a new automaton, Fanfare — you may have seen the advertisements in the newspapers — it is in the figure of a man, life-size, who plays the cornet. And there is another being developed, Labial, who plays the euphonium. I think you will understand that while I was conducting tests of the machinery, I would not have heard anything which took place in the main hall.'

Lestrade grunted acknowledgement. 'Apart from yourself and Mr Tapper, who, other than the audience, who would have been on their way out, would have been present here between ten o'clock and half past?'

'At ten o'clock, my associate Mr Cooke was on stage with me taking his bow. We have known each other since the days of our youth and were amateurs in the conjuring art long before we took it up as a profession. He constructed our first cabinet more than twelve years ago. I trust him absolutely. He usually returns home shortly after the last curtain. Then there is Mr Bromley — he is a stagehand who assists Mr Tapper and is learning the business.

'Mr and Mrs Goodgold lease the small upstairs hall for their performances and manage all their own properties. I am sure I have seen them leaving the theatre at about five or ten minutes after ten. Monsieur Gaston and his sister, and Prince Chandra and his wife, also manage their own properties, and would have left before Mr Tapper.

'Mr Campbell the Scottish Giant has this room, but he is only here between the hours of twelve and four. The box office is manned by Mr Jennings. It closes after the matinee ends at five o'clock, to enable him to record and bank the day's takings, after which he goes home.'

'That would be a substantial sum,' Lestrade observed.

'Our ledgers are available for your inspection if you require them,' said Maskelyne.

Lestrade made another note. 'Would Mr Tapper have had access to the money? He would have known when Mr Jennings was counting it and going to the bank.'

'Tapper was never concerned with the money. When Mr Jennings counted the takings, he did so behind locked doors. And he never went to the bank alone. He was always accompanied by Mr Bromley, who is his nephew and is large enough both to handle scenery with ease and deter robbers. But anyone who worked here would have known that.'

Lestrade nodded and sat back for a moment in contemplation. 'What do you think might have happened to

Mr Tapper? Who might have wanted to tie him up and why would they have done so?'

'I can only speculate on the possibilities,' said Maskelyne with a sigh. 'Tapper had claimed that he knew the secret of escaping from the rope and might stand in for me or Mr Cooke if required. Perhaps someone, a person who did not know his state of health, thought Tapper was being boastful and decided to play a trick on him. They may have asked him to demonstrate his skill and then tied him up with a rope that he could not easily slip out of. This would explain why Tapper consented to be restrained.

'The Davenport brothers were sometimes exposed by a similar trick. Volunteers tied them so well or tightly that they were unable to escape and after complaining of unfair treatment, they had to be cut free and abandon their performance. If Tapper panicked and his heart failed him, the trickster would have removed his own rope, tied the poor fellow with the usual one and left the body to be found, thinking the death would be attributed to an accident in which no-one else was involved. Of course,' Maskelyne continued, with a glance at my friend, 'he did not reckon with the appearance of Mr Holmes.' He shook his head regretfully. 'It would not be the first time a man has died trying to emulate a rope trick best left to more practised individuals, and it will almost certainly not be the last.'

'Have you ever been unable to extricate yourself?' asked Lestrade.

'No, but then I believe Mr Cooke and I are more skilled than the Davenports. If you have seen what we do, it will be obvious that we can free ourselves with ease. Also, the volunteers who tie us are not trying to expose us as frauds. We do not imply that we have supernatural assistance, on the contrary, our purpose is to demonstrate that the entire act employs nothing more than the art of the conjuror,' said Maskelyne. 'The Davenports were sometimes tied by persons who were suspicious of their reputation as mediums. There are certain knots which, when one tries to slip from the ropes, only tighten themselves further. The Tom-fool knot is a well-known one. I think that might be how they were caught out. Every escape artist who asks a volunteer to bind him must be aware of these tricks and as soon as he senses what is being attempted, take suitable action to prevent embarrassment.'

'Would it be possible, do you think, for a member of the audience, or a visitor to one of the exhibitions to remain in the building after ten o'clock if he planned to meet with Mr Tapper?' asked Lestrade.

'I perform the impossible every evening at eight, with matinees three times a week,' said Maskelyne. 'Yes, of course.'

'And would such a person be able to slip away afterwards, unnoticed?'

'If by then the only other occupant of the building was myself, and I was in the workshop, yes. The front door could still be opened from the inside and would then be closed as he departed. Only someone entering from outside would require a key.'

'Would a woman have been capable of tying Mr Tapper so he could not escape?'

'Easily. He might have been more compliant, sensing less danger.'

'A capital error,' said Holmes drily.

At that moment, we were joined by Mr Cooke who had just arrived. Cooke, noticeably shorter in stature than his friend, was in his early fifties, with a receding hairline for which he compensated by a pendulous set of side whiskers, worn beardless, in the Dundreary style. His expression showed that he had already encountered the police presence and knew that something was amiss.

Lestrade informed him of the death of Mr Tapper and the fact that it was now considered suspicious. Cooke, I thought, was less of a natural showman but a lively and willing associate whose enjoyment of the stage went a long way to endear him to the audience. Maskelyne was the gifted mechanic and charming presenter, Cooke his friend the quieter man, a reliable participator in many of the illusions. When questioned, he confirmed what we had already been told, that he had last seen Tapper when the performance ended and departed for home soon afterwards.

Lestrade closed his notebook and, commenting that the investigation would undoubtedly be placed in the hands of a more senior officer, left to make his report.

I was left contemplating the fact that the enquiry thus far had expanded the pool of suspects in the death of Mr Tapper to most of the population of London.

CHAPTER SIX

At the Egyptian Hall later that day, it was as if nothing had occurred. Tapper's body had been removed for examination by the surgeon in order to establish the cause of death, and a note from Lestrade informed us that it was hoped that the inquest would take place without delay. Before the theatre could be permitted to re-open for performances, a small deputation of police had thoroughly inspected the mysterious cabinet which I think they assumed to be full of secret compartments, mirrors and trapdoors, but was actually exactly what it seemed to be. All staff and performers had been warned to make themselves available for questioning, and not to leave London. The show was advertised and took place as usual.

Holmes had gone to the chemistry laboratory at Barts to examine the fibres he had collected of the missing rope which had bound the deceased. Since he did not require my assistance, I decided to take advantage of a free afternoon by paying a visit to the small exhibition room, where, as advertised, William Campbell, 'Her Majesty's Largest Subject', would be pleased to see the public at his levée, from twelve to four, admission 2s 6d, children half price. His tenure there was of a short duration and despite the pressure of my studies, I had to take my chance of meeting him when I could.

There I found the Scottish Giant seated very contentedly on the large settle, which had been made comfortable for him by the addition of layers of rugs; an item of furniture designed to accommodate two, but which he filled to capacity. Several curious persons occupied the chairs. He was an impressive figure, clad in full Highland dress, complete with kilt and sporran, which added to the interest of the occasion. Every item of clothing must have been tailored to his proportions — even the knitted stockings, which strained around his enormous calves.

While I could not be certain of his weight and dimensions, which are so often exaggerated by those who make their living by exhibiting themselves to the public gaze as curiosities, I saw that the advertisements had not overstated his size. He was undoubtedly a very substantial man, by far the largest I had ever seen before and indeed since. I also noticed a red rash on his lower legs, which was concerning. He greeted us in a pleasant and generous manner and said he would be pleased to answer any questions we might have.

Most of the visitors wished to know his history. He told us that he had been born in Glasgow, the second of seven children, all of whom were of the usual height and weight. His father was the same height as he, six foot four inches, although of normal build, and his mother was a more diminutive lady. He had been of unusual size since childhood, having weighed four stones before he reached his first birthday. He would attain the age of twenty-two years in April and was recently married.

There were of course many questions on the subject of his diet, and he said that he ate modest meals and did not imbibe alcoholic drinks to excess, despite the fact that he was the manager of a public house, the Duke of Wellington in Newcastle upon Tyne. He was also, he added, with a smile and a twinkle in his eye, a benefactor to society since he tested the strength of coach springs to ensure that they were safe for public use. I wondered if medicine could do anything to cure him of his weight, which I feared would shorten his life. If the cause was not the result of overconsumption of either food or drink, then I thought that something in his blood or his glands might provide a clue to the mystery.

It was obvious to me that Campbell could not be suspected of any involvement in the death of Tapper, firstly because he was not in the hall at the time, and also his size would have limited his movements, and entirely precluded him from entering the cabinet to secure the victim. Nevertheless, I wondered if he had any observations to share. Once the first group of visitors had departed, I approached him, and asked his permission as a student of surgery, to examine the red rash on his legs. He agreed, and I was sorry to see the signs of erysipelas. I gave him the appropriate advice on how to manage the condition, for which he thanked me.

'I hope they are looking after you well here,' I said.

'They are, indeed,' he replied. 'Until today, Mr Tapper was on hand to provide any assistance and refreshments I required, and now that duty has fallen to young Mr Bromley. He told me that Mr Tapper has suffered an accident,' he added.

'Yes,' I said, unsure how to proceed. 'Unfortunately, he has expired.'

'Oh, I am sorry to hear it.'

'What did you make of him?' I asked. 'It is just that the doctors are uncertain of what condition brought about his end and would welcome any information you might have. Was he well when you last saw him?'

'I thought he had a weakness about the chest,' said Campbell. 'It seemed to give him some discomfort. But that is all I know. He was active enough and made it clear that he expected a gratuity for his assistance. We talked a little about the other acts appearing here.' He paused, thoughtfully. 'There was something he said which struck me as curious.'

'Oh? What did he say?'

'I don't recall his exact words, but it was to the effect that apart from Mr Maskelyne and Mr Cooke and myself, no-one performing at the Egyptian Hall appeared before the public under his own name.'

'I understand that is quite common amongst conjurors,' I said. 'They adopt fantastical stage names to add to their air of mystery.'

'That is true; after all, I am the Scottish Giant, but I do not conceal my true name. No, Mr Tapper implied that he knew of one person here who had a great secret, and it would be very unfortunate for that individual if it was revealed. How he had come into possession of this secret he did not say. He had, however, promised that person he would not tell another soul what he knew. And when he said so, he smiled and patted his pocket.'

'You mean he was being paid for his silence?' I exclaimed.

'He did not say it in so many words, but I gathered as much.'

'Did he tell you who that individual was?'

Campbell smiled. 'I rather thought he wanted to keep that to himself.'

'Have you told anyone else about this?' I asked.

'I thought it none of my business,' he replied. 'And if I had done so he would simply have denied it. Of course, now the man is no more, I suppose you may tell who you please.'

I thanked Mr Campbell and hurried at once to Barts where, as I anticipated, I found Holmes at work in the chemistry laboratory. He was in close conference with Sergeant Lestrade and Surgeon Eastley, and at once beckoned me over.

Laid out on the bench was a short piece cut from the rope normally used in the cabinet trick, as well as a section of another type of rope, some microscope slides, and a page of notes with a drawing of the bruises on the wrists of the deceased.

'This rope, used by Maskelyne and Cooke,' said Holmes, pointing out the first sample, 'is manila hemp. Notice the pale colour and the smooth fibres. I have no doubt that the nature of the material is of great assistance in performing the escape, by whatever means it is tied. I have retrieved some fibres from the cabinet which appear to come from a different kind of rope, and this sample I have here is the nearest I could find to that type. The microscope shows the fibres to be both darker and coarser. They would tend to grip well if tied.'

Eastley nodded. 'I agree. Mr Holmes and I are of the conclusion that the material of this other rope is untreated jute. The sample and the fibres compare well.'

'Mr Eastley has kindly provided his notes which include a drawing of the marks left by a rope on the body, and a measurement of the twist pattern,' said Holmes. 'The struggles of the deceased make it hard to determine the width of the rope with any precision; however, if we compare the two ropes we have here and the twist of each, we can see that the marks are far more likely to have been left by the jute than the manila.'

'So you are saying,' said Lestrade, 'that the jute being coarser, it would have been harder to escape from than the manila.'

'For a man of little experience, that is entirely possible,' said Holmes. 'Tapper might have been confident he could emulate Maskelyne and Cooke, but I suspect that he practised the escape using their rope. And when he was tied with a different rope, he did not have the skills to overcome the difficulty.'

'As to the cause of death, it was as we thought, a failure of the heart,' said Eastley. 'It might have happened at any time, but it was brought on by fright. He was not under the influence of drink.'

'I can confirm that he did not appear at the King George Tavern that night,' said Lestrade. 'I am wondering if the whole exercise was simply the result of a boast or even a wager,' he added. 'The man or woman who secured him might not have intended any harm and may not have known Tapper's state of health or realised the dangers. If that was the case, they might successfully maintain that no crime has been committed.'

'Alternatively,' I said, 'that person was being blackmailed by Tapper. Perhaps he tied him up to teach him a lesson.'

Three pairs of eyes turned to me.

I saw at once that Holmes was giving me a warning look, one I recognised all too well, since in the past my ideas have sometimes proved to be very wide of the mark. I quickly added, 'I have just now spoken to Mr William Campbell, who exhibits between twelve and four, and until today he was assisted by Mr Tapper. He says that Tapper told him that someone appearing at the hall was not there under his real name and is concealing a secret, something he would not wish to be made public. Tapper hinted that he was receiving money for his silence.'

'That information does rather change the picture,' observed Eastley. 'The person who tied Tapper, even if he had not anticipated his death, might have done so in order to frighten him, and a charge of manslaughter could be appropriate.'

'If he had known of Tapper's weakness, and the risk of his dying from fright, and cared nothing if that was the result, then we might even be looking at a case of murder,' said Lestrade.

'Indeed so,' agreed Eastley. 'I must thank you, Mr Holmes, and you, Mr Stamford. I will see you at the inquest tomorrow.'

'Inspector Knight might want to take the lead in the investigation, in which case he will be there,' said Lestrade. 'I will make sure to brief him fully. In view of the seriousness of the situation, Mr Holmes, Mr Stamford, I will need to know where you both were on the evening of Mr Tapper's death.'

Fortunately, Holmes was at a late supper following a lecture at Barts, and I was dining with my parents. My involvement in Holmes's enquiries had placed me under suspicion more than once before, and I was thankful not to experience that embarrassment again.

Lestrade noted our replies and looked at his pocket watch. 'I think there is still time for me to speak to the Scottish gentleman,' he said, and quickly left us.

CHAPTER SEVEN

The inquest, which opened the following morning, did not hold any surprises for us, neither did it take long. The deceased was formally identified by his landlord, and the cause of death determined as heart failure. There were no suspicious injuries on the body apart from the marks of the rope, and he had not been under the influence of alcohol. The unusual circumstances of discovering the body were remarked upon, but it was established that Tapper had frequently boasted that he could emulate his employer's feat of escaping when tied and had either bound himself, or someone else had done this for him. The jute rope that had cut into his wrists was of a common type used for securing parcels. It was not, however, an item kept for general use in the Egyptian Hall, and nothing matching it had been discovered there in searches. The death was still the subject of a police enquiry, as it was thought that another person must have been present, and the circumstances were held to be suspicious, but as far as the coroner was concerned the matter could be closed.

Lestrade was there and informed us that Tapper had left little in the way of personal effects at his lodgings. There was no correspondence, and no official documents, although there were signs that old papers had been burnt. A tin box underneath his bed held some money which was rather greater than might have been expected, considering his wages. He also had a bundle of printed notices advertising theatrical performances, although he had never, as far as was known, appeared on stage. Efforts were being made to trace his next of kin.

We were introduced to Inspector Knight of Westminster Police Division, who we were told would from now on be directing the inquiry into Tapper's death. The police in those days were slow to appreciate the assistance of Sherlock Holmes, who was no more to them than a member of the public, and a student, to boot. Holmes was then just twenty-four years of age, and Knight, some ten years his senior. The youthful aspiring detective was obliged to prove himself, and earn the confidence of policemen, one by one. The inspector, however, would have heard from Lestrade's report of Holmes's examination of the body and the cabinet, and gathered that my friend's conclusions were the main reason why the death had not been recorded as an accident. As we exchanged the usual politenesses, Knight regarded Holmes with a wary interest, but there was not as yet an offer of collaboration.

As we were about to leave, a professional-looking gentleman approached us and supplied his card, revealing that he was the solicitor watching the proceedings on behalf of Messrs Maskelyne and Cooke. 'My clients would like to meet with you if that is convenient,' he said.

Holmes accepted on behalf of us both, and we once again found ourselves in the Egyptian Hall.

The meeting took place in the small exhibition gallery, and the two gentlemen greeted us warmly.

'I have had a further interview with Sergeant Lestrade, who has recommended you if I should require the services of a private enquiry agent,' Maskelyne began, 'although I was already impressed by the methodical nature of your approach when we found the body. Would you be interested in exploring this matter further? As you can imagine, the death of Mr Tapper and its possible connection to his work here is a matter of some moment to us. We have many good friends in our profession but there are also jealous rivals, and a few downright enemies.'

'I am not a professional detective,' said Holmes, 'although it is my intention to one day make it my career. I have, however, spent several years in study to ready myself for that eventuality. I do not as yet ask payment for my services. I will be pleased to assist you in any way I can. Perhaps you could begin by describing your most pressing concerns.'

The two gentlemen glanced at each other, satisfied with that reply, and Cooke gestured to indicate that he was content for his partner to take the lead.

'The profession of conjuror is unusual,' said Maskelyne, 'and I am not merely referring to the performance on stage and the skills required to create the illusion. Although many of us are known to each other and have worked together, there is another side to our interaction. Conjuring is an ancient art, and its historical methods are well-known, they are even described in manuals for those who wish to enter the profession or merely amuse themselves or entertain their friends. But when a magician devises his own illusions, and constructs his own special apparatus, he does not share this knowledge with others except under very strict conditions. Our secrets are just that, and our methods are scrupulously guarded. An entire career may be built upon a unique spectacle and will be threatened if the methods and materials used are revealed to another man who will simply copy them for his own purposes. Not everything can be protected by patent, like Psycho. My equipment and constructions are kept secure from prying eyes, and the performers I engage — who bring their properties with them — are under strict advice to take responsibility for their own materials.'

'May I take it that a successful conjuror who has his own secret methods must be on the alert for spies?' asked Holmes.

'Yes, always. Other conjurors will try to place themselves in positions to observe how illusions are achieved. They might employ confederates to work in the theatre, often as stagehands or assistants, in order to report back to them, or even steal items that can be copied. They can suborn those who are already in those positions, offering to pay well for information.'

'But you expose secrets, do you not?' said Holmes. 'You demonstrate the methods of the Davenport brothers as a part of your performance.'

Maskelyne smiled. 'I do indeed, since they perpetrated a fraud. They led the public to believe they were assisted by spirits. I maintain that their effects were produced by a simple trick. I perform the trick, but I do so merely to show that it *is* a trick. I am careful, however, not to reveal to the audience how that trick is done, since that is a secret of the professional conjuror, and it is employed by others in their performances. The spiritualists on the other hand, when they counter-attack, accuse conjurors of fraud, claiming that we are actually spirit mediums but not admitting it. Alternatively, they retaliate by exposing our secrets to the public, something no conjuror should ever do.

'There was a Mr Sexton some years ago, before we came to London, who actually published in a spiritualist journal the whole structure and dimensions of a cabinet I was then using to produce a popular illusion. It was a humorous sketch with multiple transformations, appearances and disappearances, including a gorilla. Of course, that outrage only stimulated me to devise and build a better cabinet.' He mused for a moment.

'That has not been performed for a while. I might revive it. Audiences are always amused by a gorilla.'

'Thank you, I perceive the difference,' said Holmes. 'So, may I take it that Mr Tapper's death has alerted you to the possibility that he was acting as a spy for a rival? A man who had worked for you for five years?'

'I did not suspect him, but he would have been a good target for such an approach. A trusted man who knew the premises thoroughly and operated the stage machinery. He was often involved in the testing of new work before it was perfected. His assistant, young Bromley, is simply learning the business. He is a strong pair of hands, and I had recently observed that Tapper required some help in that area. I was considering putting Tapper on lighter duties, due to his age and state of health, but he was still a valuable employee with many years of experience, and I was not about to replace him.'

'You have been made aware of what he told Mr Campbell?'

'I have. Tapper was always pleased to receive small gratuities for his work. I turned a blind eye to that. But it now seems he was also receiving payment for his silence regarding something one of the acts wished to conceal. That is disturbing. I know nothing to the detriment of any person here, but of course it might have been something not connected with their profession.'

'Have you noticed any signs that some of your secrets may have been stolen?'

'No. There have been crude copies, yes, but not my own work.'

I was emboldened to ask a question. 'Are there many men who are jealous of your success?'

'Undoubtedly, but they are often unaware of the labour involved in achieving it and wish to take a quicker way by stooping to cheap imitation and theft.'

'Or they might simply bear you malice? I am sure there are many such amongst spirit mediums. I was thinking of Mr Henry Slade, who I read about in the newspapers,' said Holmes.

Maskelyne chuckled. 'Yes, the slate-writing medium.' I must have appeared mystified, for he turned to address me. 'Imagine if you will, a slate, with no writing upon it. A fragment of chalk is placed upon it, and it is held against the underside of a table. You hear the sound of chalk writing, and when the slate is examined there appears on its surface a message from the spirits. A simple piece of conjuring, as I demonstrated when I gave evidence at Slade's trial at Bow Street. He did not relish being made to look rather foolish in public, and the fraudster that he is. I believe he has fled the country since then, and we are well rid of him. There are, however, some men,' he continued, 'and these are fortunately rare, who attack a rival's reputation by planting devices or damaging his property, to make his tricks fail on stage.'

'That could be dangerous, surely,' said Holmes.

'That is true of many illusions. But in the confined area of our small stage, and the lack of room below, I do my best to avoid the larger and more risky acts. We have no trapdoor machinery as some theatres do, since there is only a forty-inch space under the boards. I do not as a rule permit fire to be used on stage. And I do not engage performers who might be a danger to themselves or others. There are, for example, men who employ fire-eating and explosives in their acts, such as Ling Look the 'Fire-King', who presents himself as Chinese, although he is not, of course. He swallows a red-hot sword which he propels down his throat by firing a musket. Such an act, if it resulted in injury or death of the performer, or any of his assistants, or set fire to the theatre, would ruin me. I am lessee of the hall, and engage the acts, so must accept some responsibility.

'The bullet catch is another performance fraught with danger. Not many years ago a conjuror, Herr Blume, a man of considerable experience, was shot and killed on stage. I was told it was due to a lapse of attention, a failure to load the gun properly. And there was a nasty incident when a volunteer, who was asked to fire a gun at a conjuror, was killed when the gun exploded.'

'On the other hand, there is the troublesome Mr Fiz,' said Cooke, gently. 'He is not so much a danger to anyone as an annoyance.'

'Yes, indeed,' said Maskelyne. 'He must regret crossing me, but he brought it on himself. I think he is still in hiding somewhere, licking his wounds.'

'Tell me about Mr Fiz,' said Holmes.

CHAPTER EIGHT

'I feel sorry for the man,' said Maskelyne. 'He was not the primary author of his downfall. That role must be assigned to his manager, Mr Ashbury, as disreputable a character as ever worked in the profession. About a year ago, Ashbury discovered that someone was making and selling poor replicas of my automaton Psycho, a device which was designed and constructed by me over a period of more than two years. Of course, the copies were not automata at all — they contained no actual machinery — but were mere puppets which, with the guidance of a human hand, could perform amusing tricks. Ashbury, however, thought it was possible to represent these toys to less discerning audiences than attend the Egyptian Hall, as actual automata. In order to do so, however, they would need to be controlled by an individual small enough to be concealed inside the device, but old enough to perform what was required. How was he to find such a person? An adult of small stature was too robust of build to conceal himself in the box such a figure rested upon. An infant was incapable of following instructions.

'And then he chanced upon a conjuror, Oliver Fishwick, who had been training his young son, a small but intelligent boy, to assist him on stage. Soon Ashbury was advertising Fishwick as the amazing Mr Fiz, and the miraculous Osric, which greatly resembled Psycho, as a new mechanical marvel. He claimed that Osric was a genuine automaton, not controlled by a human hand — as could be proven if someone was to thrust a sword through its body. This was nonsense, of course. Osric the puppet stands upon a box rather larger than that on which Psycho stands. The child could fit inside the box and was able to move the head and hand of the figure using cues suggested by his father.

'Fishwick and son toured the land; Scotland, Liverpool, Manchester, Bristol, and were highly acclaimed wherever they were seen. At least they were praised to the rooftops in articles and letters published in newspapers which I suspect were written either by Fishwick or Ashbury. It was foolish, but they did not affect the London theatre, so I took no notice for the time being. And then Mr Ashbury started to overreach himself. He began to advertise Osric as superior to Psycho. And finally, he took a step I could not ignore. He claimed that he was the sole inventor of the mechanism of Osric, and my Psycho was merely a copy of his work.'

'You have grounds to sue for libel,' said Holmes.

'I did not care to take him to court,' said Maskelyne. 'I have my own methods. I submitted a statement to the newspapers telling Ashbury that if he was able to prove his claim, I would donate £200 to a charity, and if he could not, he should make a similar donation. I offered to send expert observers to examine Osric, the loser of the challenge to pay their expenses. He did not respond, but the publicity was sufficient to deter theatres. Of course, there were still venues which had already booked Osric and Fiz, on the strength of their earlier appearances.

'A few weeks later, as a performance commenced, a man mounted the stage carrying a walking cane and vowed to prove the truth. The cane was actually a swordstick which he drew, intending to pass it through the body of the figure, into which the boy had thrust his arm. Of course, Fishwick at once rushed up and prevented this impalement, but the fearful cries of the child were heard coming from within the box, and the secret was out. There was an immediate outcry from the audience, many of whom left their seats and invaded the stage. The box was torn open to reveal the fraud, and when the boy emerged the irate mob assaulted the puppet, and father and son fled the theatre.'

'When and where was this?' I asked.

'Last September in Weston-super-Mare. I do not believe Osric has been seen since. I think Fishwick eventually managed to carry it away, but I have been told it was badly damaged.'

'If Mr Fishwick and his son are competent conjurors, they might be able to find a new manager,' I said. 'In fact, they would be well advised to do so.'

'I hope they can. After all, they only performed what they were hired to do, and I understand they did it well. They were able to maintain the illusion before audiences. If Fishwick was to come to me asking for help, I would not engage him for the hall, but I am sure I would find some employment for him. But he must think of me as his enemy, so I doubt that he would appeal to me for assistance.'

'Have you ever met Mr Fishwick or Mr Ashbury?'

'I have not had that pleasure, although they might have visited the hall to see what else of mine they might copy. In fact, one of the performers here, Mr Goodgold, who leases the upper hall, encountered Mr Ashbury some years ago, and told me he thought he had seen the man lurking near the box office very recently.'

'I would like to speak to the other persons appearing here,' said Holmes. 'I know the police have already interviewed them, but I have my own methods of enquiry.'

'Of course. I will make sure they will speak to you, and this gallery would be a suitably private place. I should mention that all of them have been very open with the police about their location at the time of Tapper's death, and in many cases, there are witnesses to prove an alibi.'

Holmes merely nodded. 'I will also see if Tapper's landlord has anything to add.'

'For what it is worth,' interpolated Cooke, 'for all his little peccadilloes, Tapper loved what he did, he loved the hall, and he admired Mr Maskelyne. I can't imagine him willingly selling our secrets to another man.'

'But he might have been subjected to a threat,' said Holmes.

'In which case,' said Maskelyne, 'Mr Ashbury is the very first man I would suspect.'

CHAPTER NINE

Holmes sometimes gives the impression that he has leapt effortlessly to a detailed solution to a mystery, even where the facts are obscure and complicated, after nothing more than a relaxing session with his pipe. The truth of the matter is that he is supremely methodical, with a mind that sifts evidence at an incalculable speed. While he might be presented with an obvious motive for a crime, and a clear suspect, he does not instantly dismiss any facts which might not appear to fit the easy conclusion. He always examines all possibilities, even the most unlikely, and leaves no stone unturned in his search for the truth. Eliminating false trails is a tedious though essential process, and this enables him to clear his mind of distractions and address his energy in a more meaningful and effective way.

Following our interview with Maskelyne and Cooke, all possibilities leading to the death of Mr Tapper still remained open for exploration, and one route by which we could narrow the enquiry was to learn as much as we could about Mr Tapper.

Holmes was able to secure an interview with the landlord Mr Fergus, but this revealed little. The deceased stage assistant appeared to have made very little imprint on the world. Almost nothing was known of his life outside his work. He had lived in London for only a few years and all that Fergus could tell us of Tapper's history before then, was that he had once mentioned being born in Sheffield and had never married. Fergus thought there might be a female friend, but he did not know her name and had never met her.

Tapper's inquest had been reported in the newspapers, but no-one had approached Fergus either with condolences or offers of information. As far as he was concerned, all was now in the hands of the police. Careful questioning by Holmes revealed little more. The only thing Tapper talked about freely was his working life. His love of theatre began in boyhood, and he had sought stage work as soon as he was able. He started by running errands, taking messages, helping with props, and gradually gaining a knowledge of scenery and apparatus.

'Did he ever speak about the performers he had worked with?' asked Holmes. 'Magicians in particular. The theatres that employed him? The places he had visited?'

'He was at Crystal Palace when he first came to London, that was before he started at the Egyptian Hall,' said Fergus. 'I think he did the special fancy effects for the pantomimes. That was where he met Mr Maskelyne. Before that, he mainly worked at theatres in places like Sheffield, Bristol, Liverpool. There were some handbills amongst his things. I gave them to the police.'

'He never went abroad?'

'He never said he had. The only magician he mentioned was a Professor something, I forget his name, Wizard of the North, he called himself, but when he went off to tour the world, Tapper didn't go with him. That must have been when he came to London.'

I could see that Holmes was thoughtful and I knew from the little movement of his fingertips that he would very much like to examine the material currently in the hands of the police and could imagine the papers already in his grasp.

After considering these few meagre facts, Holmes's conclusion was that no theory of Tapper's demise could be excluded. He was not yet ready to rule out the possibility that the tragedy was the result of a foolish and careless prank.

While in the Egyptian Hall, Tapper was undoubtedly in a position to be entrusted with or acquire secrets, secrets which were valuable, and had the potential to make or destroy a career. Maskelyne, the constructor of unique apparatus, would have been a prime target for copying and theft. If Tapper had been restrained by someone in an effort to cajole him into revealing Maskelyne's secrets, then this might have been the act either of a rival conjurer or a determined spiritualist, furious at repeated assaults on the reputation of the still-revered Davenport brothers.

Studying the history of the legendary Davenports, told us not only about the brothers and their adherents, but also provided further insights into their adversary, Maskelyne, his strength, courage and ingenuity, and the enmity he had attracted by his boldness and unflinching dedication to unmask fraud.

In 1865, Americans Ira and William Davenport, hailed as the world's greatest demonstrators of spiritual powers, had, while touring Britain, been publicly exposed as charlatans by Maskelyne and Cooke. The two then amateur conjurors had been invited on stage to witness a Davenport exhibition in their home town of Cheltenham. Once the brothers had been tied inside the cabinet and the doors bolted, all lights were extinguished, and dark blinds drawn across the windows.

During the performance it so chanced that one of the blinds inexplicably moved aside, admitting enough light for Maskelyne and Cooke to perceive that the wonders taking place were created by the brothers after slipping their bonds. Other men finding themselves in possession of the true state of affairs might have waited until the performance had ended and had a quiet word with the brothers or their manager, or written an anonymous letter to the newspapers. Not so Messrs Maskelyne and Cooke, who seized the moment.

Leaping fearlessly from their seats, they openly denounced the Davenports as tricksters, which led to an uproar and a cessation of the performance. It was obvious, however, that mere words were not enough to prove their point. Attacked on every side by the Davenports' devoted supporters, the two as yet inexperienced men took a bold course. They set about constructing their own 'Cabinet of Wonders' and familiarised themselves with the escape trick. Some weeks later they held a demonstration and invited the public to attend. Hundreds of onlookers saw them prove their claim, by performing every detail of the Davenports' act with skill and panache.

One might imagine that such a destruction of the basic principle that drew the crowds to supposed mediums would end the brothers' fame, but such was the Davenports' hold over the hearts and minds of their believers, it made very little difference. The only detectable result was their determination never to tour Britain again.

Believers continued to hold that the brothers were accomplished mediums, and defended them vociferously, castigating British audiences for acting out of anti-American prejudice. The public, whether searching for enlightenment or the spectacle of a dramatic exposure, flocked to their subsequent appearances. Their career was only ended by the death of one brother in 1877, leading to the retirement of the other, but by then, there were numerous copyists. The notorious cabinet had by then become a potent symbol of the conjuror's art: closed doors behind which mysteries and transformations could be enacted, the excitement of the audience mounting as they anticipated each dramatic revelation.

Maskelyne's pursuit of frauds remained relentless, and any mediums who arrived to ply their business in London were in danger of their performances being observed and satirised to devastating effect at the Egyptian Hall. The most recent arrival was a man called Prospero, who used not a cabinet, but a black curtain drawn across the corner of a room to conjure an assortment of ghosts from the murky recesses. I suspected that his tenure of the London scene would be short-lived.

Maskelyne was no fool, he knew that by his actions he was making enemies, the only question was how dangerous these enemies were, and how far they would go in opposition.

Without the authority of the police, or any official standing, Holmes and I had only one approved means of delving further into the mystery of Mr Tapper's death, the permission of Mr John Nevil Maskelyne to interview all those employed in the Egyptian Hall. We were able to appropriate the gallery during the interval between the Scottish Giant's departure and the start of the evening performance, and there we waited to see what realities lay beneath the outer appearances.

Our first interview was with His Highness Prince Chandra the magician, exponent of the great mysteries of the East, including the world-famous Indian basket trick. Mr Norman Chandler, as he was known when not regaling audiences with his exotic wonders, came to see us in the company of his associate, Princess Yasmin, or Mrs Evie Chandler, who I was relieved to see was rather more modestly clad than on stage. I appreciated that Mr Chandler, an Englishman aged about thirty, must employ an application of suitable greasepaint to his face to make his masquerade as Indian royalty more convincing. Mrs Chandler, a natural beauty in her twenties, with lustrous dark hair, required no such artifice.

'I represent myself in Indian style, as I perform the mysteries of that continent,' said Chandler. 'My late father was a minor official who served in India for ten years, and all the family lived there during that time. From childhood I was fascinated by the popular illusions I saw performed. These were shown in the open air, where there was no possibility of concealed devices, employing the simplest of materials, and yet were thrilling to behold. They form some of my most powerful and engaging memories.

'There is a rich and wonderful history of conjuring in India. If one looks at many of the illusions being performed on stage in Britain, Europe, and America, one can see that so many of the ideas and techniques have their roots in India. I was never able to comprehend how the tricks were done, and that set me on the course which has brought me here.

'The basket trick is simple yet beautiful if performed well. I once saw a man place his servant boy in a basket which was then sawn in half in front of our eyes. How we shuddered at the screams of agony! How we dreaded what might be found inside! A shawl was thrown over what we believed must be the hideous remains and then, to our astonishment, the servant reappeared unharmed in the crowd of onlookers. And here was the great innovation of the trick; there were two of them dressed the same — identical twins. He had made two out of one.' He uttered a wistful sigh. 'If Evie had a twin sister, I am sure I would attempt it myself.'

'And the famous rope trick?' I asked.

He chuckled indulgently, and his wife smiled. 'That is India's greatest mystery,' she said.

'Yes, it is the stuff of legend,' said Chandler. 'Many will speak of it, but no-one has seen it. Not in the fullest form as is so often claimed. But since you mention it, I intend to develop an entertainment along those lines. Imagine if you will, a coil of rope lying on the stage. Spellbinding music plays, and one end of the rope rises like a cobra about to strike.' He gestured in demonstration, his arms waving like snakes. 'Higher and higher it goes, up and up, until the rope is straight as a column and the top cannot be seen.'

I guessed, of course, that the rope must be drawn up by a thread, but did not say so.

'And then,' he exclaimed, 'I conjure Princess Yasmin to climb the rope.' He was not holding a wand, but his gestures were so refined and graceful that one could easily imagine one in his hand. 'As I raise the wand higher, so she climbs and climbs, until she is hidden from the view of the audience.' He stared upwards towards the ceiling. 'And now I pretend that she has vanished. The audience is amused. I pretend to be annoyed and command her to come down. Then — what horror!' He gasped. 'A figure falls to the stage! The audience cries out. The shock is powerful! What, they wonder, has happened to the lovely Princess Yasmin? Is she alive or dead? Should someone call a doctor?' His features abruptly changed from horror to amusement. 'I turn to them and indicate that I am not alarmed, I can make all well with my wand. I take a cloak and place it over the motionless body. I wave my wand. The music plays, and slowly the cloak rises; it is thrown aside and there is Princess Yasmin, alive and uninjured. The audience applauds mightily.'

I stared at Mrs Chandler, who did not appear to be concerned at being required to undertake this acrobatic feat. Her hands were ungloved and folded in her lap. They looked strong and capable.

'Have you performed this?' asked Holmes.

'Not yet; it is to be perfected,' Chandler admitted. 'And I think the dimensions of the stage of the Egyptian Hall will not permit it, so it must wait for a more suitable venue.'

'I look forward to seeing it,' said Holmes. 'But now to the subject of this discussion.'

'Ah, yes, the unfortunate Mr Tapper,' said Chandler.

'How well were you acquainted with him?' asked Holmes. He looked enquiringly from one to the other.

They exchanged glances. 'Hardly at all,' said Chandler. 'We had never seen him before we came here.'

'We saw him about the place doing his work,' said Mrs Chandler.

'I am not sure we ever had occasion to speak to him,' said Chandler. 'We manage our own props and a few decorative items on stage, but he was never involved with that.'

'How long is your engagement here?'

'Two months, of which we have completed the first.'

'Do you know if he might have had — perhaps enemies is too strong a word — if he had ever caused any inconvenience or upset to anyone? Had he quarrelled with someone?'

'No, not at all,' said Chandler. 'I never heard anyone object to him or criticise his work.'

'Have you ever seen him try and emulate the rope escape?'

'I was told he claimed to be able to, but I never saw it.'

Mrs Chandler nodded in agreement. 'Many men boast of what they can do, but you never see them do it,' she said.

'Did no-one suggest a challenge or a wager?'

'Not that I am aware,' said Chandler.

'Did you ever see him in conversation with someone who did not work at the hall? Someone you did not recognise?'

Both gave some thought to this, and both shook their heads.

'Did he ever indicate by word or gesture to you or anyone else that he expected to receive a gratuity or payment of any kind?'

'Not to us. I can't speak for others.'

Holmes paused. 'I understand,' he said carefully, 'that Mr Tapper was heard to make a comment to the effect that there was someone working here who had a secret in his or her past which would cause them some difficulty if it was revealed.'

'I have yet to meet anyone in this profession who does not have secrets,' said Chandler. As he spoke, he glanced at his wife once more. 'But we have nothing to say on that matter. We never spoke to Tapper on that or any other subject. We had nothing to do with his death, and we don't know who did.'

The crux of the matter was in the open. Holmes thanked them and they departed.

CHAPTER TEN

Mr and Mrs Jonathan Goodgold were a devoted couple, both of whom appeared to have been born to take the stage. Mr Goodgold, of that indeterminate age hovering in the region of forty, was slender, pale and elegant. One could readily imagine him delivering an impressive Hamlet. He could, however, turn his talents in many directions.

By the simple expedient of attaching a beard to his chin, he portrayed the late Charles Dickens so perfectly that it seemed as though some miracle had brought that gentleman back to vibrant life. Thus arrayed, he gave some of the author's most amusing and thrilling readings, with a virtuosity which moved his audiences to both laugh and weep. He and Mrs Goodgold, a buxom lady with a bright smile and sparkling eyes, performed a comedic interlude, in which a gentleman, having imbibed a little more than he ought, came home at a late hour to his disgruntled wife. The discovery of a lady's scented glove and a tender note in his coat pocket led to some humorous moments, before it was revealed that he had accidentally picked up the coat of another man, and all was harmoniously forgiven.

Mrs Goodgold was able to trill a pretty tune, following which her husband conducted an interesting conversation with a grey and white cat. When we spoke to them, the cat was nestled on Mr Goodgold's lap. It was a remarkably lifelike puppet called Archie, and such an intelligent-looking creature, that it was only slightly disconcerting when it occasionally answered our questions on its owner's behalf.

'It was the world of the theatre that brought us together,' said Goodgold. 'We were both performing as individuals, and one day by some miracle we were both in Leeds, where we appeared on the same bill, and as soon as we met, our destiny was apparent. We will have been united in marital harmony four years this April.'

'And you have been leasing the small theatre here for — how long?' asked Holmes.

'This is the fourth week of eight. Prior to that we were in Edinburgh.'

'And during your career, had either of you met Mr Tapper before now?'

'I am not aware of having seen him before we came here,' said Mrs Goodgold.

'I am sure I have never met him before,' said Mr Goodgold. 'And I am afraid I can tell you very little about him. I saw him about the place, of course, and he appeared to know his business very well, and needed no instruction. But he was mainly concerned with the large hall. The little space we have we can manage perfectly ourselves. It is simply a platform for our endeavours, and a few simple properties nicely arranged are all we require.'

'Where are your possessions stored?' asked Holmes.

'There is a little dressing space behind the back curtain, and a make-up table. The properties, once we are finished for the night, are locked in a trunk. There are a few small pieces of furniture which are of no value.'

'And Mr Tapper did not assist you with those?'

'No,' said Mrs Goodgold, 'we prefer to arrange our own things.'

'Tapper never came up here?'

'He might have done, as a part of his general duties,' said Goodgold. He stroked the cat's head. 'Did you ever see him, Archie?'

'No, I never did,' said the cat puppet.

'There you are,' said Goodgold.

'Once your evening performance was ended, what time did you leave the theatre?'

Goodgold smiled. 'When our work is done, knowing there is a warm fire and a nice supper at our lodgings, we have perfected our tidying methods so we can leave in ten minutes. Our lodgings are a mile from here. I can provide the address if you wish. The landlady will confirm our time of arrival.'

'Thank you,' said Holmes, and a slip of paper was handed over. 'If you did not speak to Mr Tapper directly, you might have been told something about him which has a bearing on his death. Did you ever hear that he had quarrelled with anyone?'

'No; in fact, I cannot recall that he was ever the subject of conversation with another person.'

'I don't think I was told anything about him other than his name,' said Mrs Goodgold.

'I have been informed that he claimed to know someone here who had a secret that was not to be revealed. Have you heard anything to that effect? If not from Tapper then from anyone else?'

Goodgold appeared taken aback by this question. 'No-one has volunteered anything of that sort to me,' he said, and glanced at the puppet. 'What about you, Archie?'

'People don't tell me any secrets,' said Archie. 'And curiosity is bad for cats.'

'I try not to pry into the business of others,' said Goodgold. 'The theatrical profession may conceal many secrets, and it does not do to ask questions.'

'But there might have been gossip,' Holmes persisted. 'Some idle talk you could have overheard. It might have meant nothing at the time, but perhaps you would oblige me by giving that some thought and see if anything comes to mind.'

'I shall certainly do so,' said Goodgold.

Mrs Goodgold agreed. 'We are here for another month, before we move on to Southend, but I promise to listen carefully in case I learn something.'

'Mr Maskelyne mentioned to me that you saw a man called Ashbury at the box office here recently,' said Holmes. 'A man who recently claimed in public to be the inventor of an automaton called Osric, and denounced Psycho as a copy. Mr Maskelyne has never met the man, but it appears that you have. You warned Mr Maskelyne about him, as you suspected he might be up to no good. Has he ever acted as your manager?'

'I am pleased to say he has not,' said Goodgold, very firmly. 'His methods are deplorable. I know that advertising can sometimes romanticise the truth and load extravagant praise where it may not be entirely due, but Mr Ashbury does not shrink from telling outright lies. Yes, the debacle over his supposed automaton, Osric, was in the theatrical papers, and he narrowly avoided a prosecution.'

'Where have you met him before?'

'Oh, it was several years ago, before I met my dear wife. He was managing two conjurors at the time, one of whom was on the same variety bill as I.' He turned to Mrs Goodgold. 'Selina, my dear — you have never met him, have you?'

'No, I have not. And from what I have heard said of him, I have been very fortunate.'

'Did you ever see Tapper in conversation with Ashbury, or anyone else who does not work here?'

'No, but I would not be surprised if Ashbury had tried to inveigle Tapper into his business. Ashbury likes to prowl about the theatres hoping to steal ideas from others. He is quite shameless about it. He has been handing out his cards here, hoping to attract performers into his fold. I warned people to avoid him. I saw him, recently, in the foyer when I was distributing leaflets — a duty we performers all share. He had changed little in appearance over the years, perhaps greyer, more heavyset, but by one thing I knew him for certain. A wheezing of the chest. Some old affliction. I heard him behind me, and when I dared to look, it confirmed my suspicion. If you should ever encounter him, he wears a Tyrolean hat. Fortunately, he did not notice me, but I have no doubt that he was here to watch the performances. Not for pleasure, but to see if he could learn the secrets of the conjurors and copy any successful acts. I don't believe the man ever had an original idea. He takes them from others and then claims them as his own. That is why I informed Mr Maskelyne, to put him on his guard. Ashbury is a man to be avoided.'

To my great surprise, Monsieur Armand Gaston, the master of legerdemain, proved to be exactly what he claimed to be — a Frenchman. He was able to use his perfect grooming and sleek good looks to full advantage on stage. In conjuring, distracting the audience from detecting trickery can be accomplished not only with sleight of hand, but with smiles, charm and a flirtatious tilt of the eyebrow.

He was accompanied by his sister Amelie, who, I discovered, presented as the human serpent, Yamadaya. She was dressed in a plain silk gown with a pretty lace collar framing a delicate face. I felt impelled to compliment her on her performance, and she smiled modestly. The black mamba costume in which she took the stage had, she confided, been specially designed for her. It enclosed her whole body like a glove, rendering her as supple and slender as a young tree, her form appearing both less and more than human. It included a hood which she drew over her head and hair. This included a gauzy face covering, which she was able to see through, and disguised the obvious femininity of her features. I confess to being an admirer of fine blue eyes, and Mademoiselle Gaston was well provided in that respect.

In common with the other performers, the Gastons told us they had not met Thomas Tapper before starting their season at the Egyptian Hall six weeks previously, neither did they need to call upon his services. They did not use large equipment in their acts, and some of the materials employed were delicate and required careful transport and storage.

When questioned on the claim that some performers at the Egyptian Hall were concealing secrets, they glanced at each other. A moment passed, then Amelie nodded to her brother. He patted her hand and turned to us.

'I will be open with you and tell you our story.'

The Gastons, who were aged twenty-seven and twenty-three respectively, had been born and brought up in Paris, where their widowed father was a prominent hotelier. He had managed one of the great fashionable houses in the city, the Hôtel Élégance, which enjoyed an international reputation and attracted distinguished visitors. The hotel, in addition to providing the best of food, wine and accommodation, also staged entertainments, and these had included performances by the premier conjurors of the day. Like Mr Chandler, the Gastons had, as children, been excited to see master magicians, and young Armand especially had devoted himself to emulating their skills. Well educated, both were competent in the English language.

'I was fifteen years of age when it all ended,' said Gaston with a sigh. 'We were too young to be told all the facts. Some of them we only learned many years later. It was a public scandal. Our father was arrested and tried for embezzlement. He was found guilty and imprisoned. The family fortunes were gone. Amelie and I were placed in the care of a widowed aunt, Madame Gaston, the sister of our late mother, who ran a small café. She was kind to us but struggled with the new burden on her resources. I offered to attract customers by performing legerdemain to amuse diners at the tables, and it was a success. Amelie, who had previously been given dance lessons, had already discovered an unusual suppleness of her joints, and was able to achieve some remarkable bodily contortions, which earned her the soubriquet of 'serpent girl'. In time, she was allowed under the careful protection of our aunt, to dance for her dinner. A manager who dined at the café saw us and offered to take us on tour.'

Holmes was thoughtful as he listened to their story. I was reminded that according to Mr Campbell, Tapper had said that the person with the secret was not appearing at the Egyptian Hall under his or her own name.

This had not escaped Holmes's notice, for he asked, 'When you took the stage as professional performers, under what name did you appear?'

'Ah, well, that was a little difficult, as you may imagine,' Gaston admitted. 'Our family name is Debrassie. My father's downfall was well known, since a great many people lost large sums of money in that affair. The name became notorious and might not have been well received. Nowadays, in England, and years after the event, it is of less moment. Initially, we performed in France as Monsieur Magique and Amelie. I was obliged to amend my name later when I found that there was another man with that title, and so we took the surname of the aunt who brought us up. And our manager suggested that Amelie adopt something with a mysterious sound.'

'Supposing,' said Holmes, 'someone was now to make public your true identity and the situation of your unfortunate father? Would that harm your standing?'

Gaston shook his head. 'We were children at the time of the scandal,' he said. 'We knew nothing of our father's crimes. Today, I think we might excite pity and possibly even admiration for having made an honest living despite suffering such a tragedy. We no longer fear exposure.'

'Did anyone ever approach you threatening such an exposure? Demanding payment for silence?'

'No. And if anyone had, I would not have submitted to such a threat.'

'Can you suggest who might have wished harm to Mr Tapper?'

'No. We meant him no ill, and if we knew who was responsible for his death we would already have told the police.'

Our next interview was with box office manager Mr Jennings. He was a gentleman in his middle fifties, thin and spare, with round steel-rimmed spectacles, and a suitably tidy appearance which he wore like a uniform. He had occupied that position ever since the Egyptian Hall had opened as a theatre. While he had occasionally seen evening performances, he had never been tempted to appear on stage.

Holmes asked him if he was aware of Mr Tapper's monetary demands, and he bridled a little, as if his own honesty was being questioned.

'Money is a very serious and sensitive subject,' said Mr Jennings. 'I hold a position of trust and have undertaken it without complaint. Whatever arrangements Mr Tapper might have made with other persons, in the form of gifts or gratuities, were his own business, and did not in any way affect the income at the box office, or the payment of wages and expenses, all of which are meticulously recorded.'

'Did he ever mention to you anyone working here, especially someone performing under a professional name, who he thought had a secret which that individual would prefer not to be revealed?'

'Tapper would never have taken me into his confidence on such a subject,' said Jennings, firmly. 'Had he done so, I would have told him to keep his silence, and not trouble me about it. Who knows if any of these tales of scandal that go about in theatres are true or false? It is better not to listen.'

'I take it you did not work with Mr Tapper?'

'No, not at all.'

'Is there anything you can tell me about him that might cast some light on his death? Did he ever meet with people who do not work here?'

'I am really unable to tell you any more than I already have. I know of no such meetings.'

Holmes nodded. 'Very well, I have no further questions. I should like to speak to Mr Bromley next. He is your nephew, I am told?'

'Yes, Peter is a good boy; young, but very steady. He has been here less than a year, but he is capable and makes himself useful.'

'Could you ask him to come and see me?'

Mr Jennings paused. 'I will, but before you speak to Peter, you should know something of his history. You are medical men, and I know you will understand. However, what I am about to tell you is in strict confidence.'

'Of course,' said Holmes.

Mr Jennings' voice, so controlled when he spoke about his work, was softer when speaking of his young nephew. 'Peter is the only child of my late sister. She made a bad marriage to a man who only valued his possessions and his dignity. When the child was born...' He sighed. 'I was told that the cord was twisted about the infant's neck, and it took time to release it and for him to take his first breath. We were informed it might affect his development, and so it proved. Peter is not as able as other children, and yet, I only wish his father had had even half the kindness and half the humanity of his son. My sister told me that her husband treated Peter with coldness and indifference. As soon as Peter was old enough, he was sent away. I was told he was at school. My sister sadly died after giving birth to her second child, a daughter, and within a few months her widowed husband remarried. When I made enquiries about my nephew, I discovered to my great horror that he was not, as I had been informed, in a school, but an asylum for the insane. I applied at once to the father for permission to remove the boy, who was then eight years of age, and take him into my care, and he agreed at once.

'Peter has lived with me ever since. He is gentle and good-natured. I taught him his letters; I taught him his numbers. I taught him to look after himself. He enjoys the society of others, and he is strong and willing to work. I know I will not always be here for him, so I have put aside some savings for when he is older. The one thing I can say with confidence is that Peter has never harmed another living being. I thought that the position of stagehand would suit him, but before he was introduced to Mr Maskelyne, I revealed his history. I concealed nothing. Mr Maskelyne was very good, and after speaking to Peter he agreed to employ him. He has never regretted that decision.'

'I assume your nephew's history is not generally known?'

'No, but why should it be? The other acts, they come and go, and it is no business of theirs. Mr Cooke knows, of course. And Tapper, whatever he was told, was more than content with an assistant who was hard working, quiet and biddable. I will fetch Peter now.'

Mr Peter Bromley was aged about twenty, tall, and solidly composed. Holmes was especially eager to question him since he had worked more closely with Tapper than anyone else at the Egyptian Hall.

'Please be seated, Mr Bromley,' said Holmes as the youth stood before us. 'I expect you know that we are speaking to everyone here to try and discover more about Mr Tapper.'

Bromley nodded.

'What are your duties here?'

'I help with the scenery, and setting out the stage, and I do what cleaning is needed during the day. I always clean after the matinee, because the children come in with their sweets. And I guard the money when my uncle takes it to the bank. That is very important.'

'You were Mr Tapper's assistant?'

'Yes. He said I was his other set of hands. For fetching and carrying. Because I am strong.'

'I have been told that Mr Tapper asked the performers to tip him. Is that the case?'

'I think so, yes.'

'Did he have any other means of earning a little extra money?'

'He sometimes said he had other business, but he never said what it was,' said Bromley. 'Kept it all to himself.'

'Was there anyone here he distrusted, or disliked, or had a quarrel with?'

'I don't know. He never told me those sorts of things. He just told me what I had to do.'

'Did he mention anyone working here who he thought had something to hide?'

Bromley thought about it. 'He once said there were a lot of people who had secrets they didn't want other people to know. But he didn't say who they were.'

'Did you know that he was in poor health?'

'He wasn't too well sometimes. Just old age, I suppose,' Bromley added with a shrug. 'I sometimes saw him rub his chest and his arm. I did ask him once if he wanted a rest and he said it was nothing.'

'Did he ever tell you that he could escape from the ropes in the cabinet like Maskelyne and Cooke?'

Bromley smiled. 'Yes, he told me that when I first came here. I think he told everyone. Very proud of that, he was.'

'Did he ever ask you to tie him up so he could show you he could free himself?'

'He did, yes, and I thought I did it properly, but he escaped really quick. Like magic, it was. He knew his business. He said he'd show me the secret of it one day, but he never did.'

'When did you last see him? You must have been working with him on the night he died.'

'Yes. I had a bit of the heavy work to do, and then Tapper said I could go early. He said he just wanted to look about before he left. So I went. I don't know what time it was. The policeman asked me that. I can tell the time, but I didn't think to look.'

'You went straight home?'

'No. I stopped at the chop house for my supper. It was a good supper. I had a shilling to spend. The policeman asked me about that as well.'

'And after your supper, did you go home?'

'Yes.'

'Apart from Mr Tapper, was there anyone else in the hall at the time you left?'

'I think Mr Maskelyne was in his workshop.'

'If Mr Tapper wanted to meet someone in private for some of his other business, would he have been able to admit them to the hall?'

'He would, yes.'

'Without Mr Maskelyne being aware of it?'

'When Mr Maskelyne is in his workshop, what with all the music and the machines, he wouldn't have heard anything.'

'Did you ever see Mr Tapper meeting with anyone about his other business? Have you heard him mention any names?' asked Holmes.

Bromley shook his head. 'No.'

'I am sure you know that there are many persons who would like to know some of Mr Maskelyne's secrets, so they can profit by them,' said Holmes. 'Either that or they are simply jealous of his success. Then there are spiritualists who are angry with him at his exposure of their methods.'

'Oh, there are,' said Bromley, nodding emphatically. 'Mr Tapper told me to look out for them and not tell them anything.'

'Did Mr Tapper know Mr Maskelyne's secrets?' asked Holmes.

'I think he knew a lot of them, because it was what he needed to know to help with things on stage. But the machines, and how they were made, that was all down to Mr Maskelyne. Mr Maskelyne is always building new things as well as working on the old ones to make them better.'

'Will you take over Mr Tapper's duties now?'

'Not yet. I think Mr Cooke will have to step in until I can learn more. He can turn his hand to anything.'

Following this series of interviews, I asked Holmes if he thought that all those we had spoken to were being truthful. 'I sense that much is being left unspoken,' he said, 'and there is at least one individual who is undoubtedly concealing something of importance. I just require the means to extract the truth.'

'They all appear to have satisfied the police as to their whereabouts,' I said.

'That was why I did not question them deeply on the subject,' said Holmes. 'The evidential value of an alibi provided by a relative or a servant is well known.'

CHAPTER ELEVEN

The inquest on Thomas Tapper had been fully reported in the newspapers, with additional commentary giving special emphasis on the unusual position of the corpse, not all of which was accurate. Lengthy editorials followed, devoted to the dangers resulting from persons who were not adept in the art of escaping from ropes tying themselves up out of bravado. Friends of such boastful individuals were warned not to agree to tie them up for amusement, especially when drink had been taken. The humorous tone of some of the letters which followed was not, I thought, in the best of taste, given the tragic outcome of some notable adventures. One correspondent recalled a Mr Leatherbarrow who claimed that he could perform the Davenport escape. He had asked some friends to suspend him from a tree by his legs, wagering that he could free himself and arrive at a nearby public house before they did. When he did not appear, they returned to the tree, to find that his struggles to free himself had caused the rope to slip and close about his neck with fatal results. Even professionals were not exempt from accident. Many years before, an American exhibition diver called Scott had perished while performing a rope feat on Waterloo Bridge. A crowd of several thousand had watched him die.

It was to be expected that dedicated spiritualists would use Tapper's death to criticise Mr Maskelyne. An entrenched enemy was especially scathing in the next issue of *The Spiritualist*, which was reprinted for comment in the theatrical newspaper, *The Era*.

For some years past a debate has raged in the popular press and scholarly journals such as The Spiritualist *concerning the tricks or otherwise of Messrs Maskelyne and Cooke who currently exhibit at the Egyptian Hall. Some who have observed these performances have declared those gentlemen to be powerful mediums although they themselves utterly deny it, saying that they are merely conjurors. Others denounce them as common tricksters. Articles and diagrams have frequently been published showing precisely how these tawdry tricks have been carried out and their cabinets constructed.*

Maskelyne and Cooke have had the effrontery to assert that because they can imitate the accomplishments of the Davenport brothers by trickery then it must necessarily follow that the feats of the Davenports must also be brought about by trickery. This conclusion does not accord with natural logic and has passed the bounds of both truth and decency. These gentlemen even inform their gaping crowds that they live in bodily fear from the violence of exasperated spiritualists. Pshaw!

But now with this recent horrible fatality, the truth has become apparent. Maskelyne and Cooke are without doubt mediums, but they operate under the guise of conjurors, and deny their true nature.

Why is this? I maintain that they deny spiritualism only to curry favour with the ignorant public. Spiritualism, as Dr Sexton has proven to us in his lectures, is a science and should be studied as such. It has however long been denied and despised by the ill-educated masses, the very persons who flock to the Egyptian Hall. Maskelyne and Cooke do not wish to associate themselves with the glories of spiritualism but prefer to make their fortunes by stooping to claims of common trickery.

But now, their wicked ways have found them out, and has resulted in the death of one of their own employees. Mr Thomas Tapper was a stagehand, a plain man who has worked at the Egyptian Hall for five years. He was not a medium, and seduced by the claim that the escape could be performed without the aid of spirits, he attempted to emulate the rope escape by his own means. In doing so he expired. For their encouragement of that belief and negligence I maintain that it is high time that Messrs Maskelyne and Cooke were arrested and charged with manslaughter.

Algernon Jones

We called upon Mr Maskelyne to report on the results of our interviews and found him in a small dressing room with his copy of *The Era*, reading Mr Jones's letter, which did not appear to discomfit him.

'Do the spiritualists come to see your performances?' asked Holmes.

'They do, I know some of them well by sight. I am sure that some of those who volunteer to tie us in the cabinet are spies. Of course, it would not benefit their cause to try and prevent us from performing our act. Some write letters to the press denouncing me and calling me a trickster. Of course, in one sense, I am a trickster. I am a conjurer. Mystifying the audience is my profession.'

He tossed the newspaper aside. 'I can assure you I am not afraid of spiritualists. They are only violent with words. They use me to give publicity to their beliefs. In doing so, they act as a recommendation, and bring the curious to see me perform.'

'Do you think spiritualists might have tried to bribe or even force Tapper to give them your secrets?'

'I doubt it. And even if they knew as much as Tapper knew, they would still not have everything. Far from it. They have tried to damage me ever since I exposed the Davenports, and they must know by now that they are tilting at a very substantial windmill.'

We went on to advise Mr Maskelyne of the results of our interviews, to which he gave careful consideration. 'I can confirm that Mr Jennings spoke to me about his nephew before introducing him to me. Mr Bromley is a reliable young man and has given every satisfaction in his work. Tapper knew that he was a little slower than others in his understanding, but it was not necessary to inform him or anyone else of Bromley's cruel and unjustified placing in an asylum when he was a mere child.'

'In any case, Tapper's comment that the person with secrets who was paying him for his silence was not here under his real name. That cannot apply to Mr Bromley,' said Holmes.

'That is the case.'

We were about to take our leave when Maskelyne, with a troubled expression, asked us to remain, saying that he wished to speak to us further on a sensitive matter. I saw Holmes's mouth twitch in anticipation of hearing something less mundane than he had been contemplating thus far.

'I don't know if this is relevant to what happened to poor Tapper,' said Maskelyne, 'but I believe that we may be harbouring a spy who has found a way to discover some of Psycho's secrets. As you must know, there is a great deal of debate amongst interested parties as to how Psycho is able to do what he does. Some speculation has come close, especially when offered by gentlemen with expertise in engineering, but so far no-one has found all that may be found.'

'What makes you think there is a spy?' asked Holmes. 'Has anyone seen a stranger in the building? Someone who has wandered where he ought not to be? Or perhaps one of the volunteers you invite on stage has been taking a closer interest than most?'

'No, we are always watchful for intruders, or suspicious behaviour. This relates to our recent matinees. Psycho is a great favourite in the afternoon performances, when families attend with their children. The program is a little different from that in the evening. There is nothing too alarming, of course, and not all parents would wish their young children to be entertained with a game of whist. But Psycho can do arithmetic or guessing a card. In the last two matinees, not all has gone to plan. Psycho has sometimes failed to respond, or even made errors. I have tried to laugh it off, and rebuked him gently, but after the performance, I have examined the mechanism very carefully and I can find no fault.'

'And you say Psycho operates as usual in the evening performances?' asked Holmes.

'There is never any difficulty with those.'

'These errors never took place before the death of Mr Tapper?'

'No. I suppose now we have one less man of experience to keep watch, which may be the root of the problem. Tapper has proved to be hard to replace.'

'Where is Psycho normally kept?' asked Holmes.

'After the evening performance he is brought to my workshop and held under lock and key. He does not come out again until half an hour before the matinee.'

'And between the matinee and the evening?'

'He is backstage, behind the rear curtain. As you may imagine, the premises are kept secure once the matinee audience has left at five o'clock,' said Maskelyne. 'The only part of the theatre available to the public at that time is the foyer. The doors to the auditorium are closed and do not re-open until half past seven. Both Mr Cooke and I have looked for any signs of an intruder and I asked Mr Bromley to carry out an inspection, but nothing suspicious has been found.'

Holmes was thoughtful. 'I agree this is a matter of concern, and suggests an intrusion rather than mechanical failure. If you would permit me, I would like to remain in the theatre after the next matinee. Would you allow myself and Mr Stamford to have the whole space to ourselves, to perform our own examination, and enjoy complete freedom of movement?'

'Certainly, that can be arranged.'

'And let no-one else know. No-one. This must be between us only. Before we do so, however, I wish to have a tour of the stage, and all exits and entrances. And I will require a closer look at Psycho.'

Maskelyne consulted his watch. 'It is now two o'clock. I will have Psycho brought out and Mr Cooke will watch over him while we tour the premises. And please accept two tickets for the performance.'

We began our tour by inspecting the doors which admitted the audience, and the passages and stairs leading to the seating, all of which could be made secure. There was separate access for the performers, and storage for the scenery and larger properties, as well as small spaces employed as dressing rooms.

The area behind the back curtain was just wide enough for two persons to pass, and here we found Mr Cooke cheerfully polishing the glass cylinder on which Psycho normally rested. The low wooden stand was separate; however, the little figure in his bright silken garments and turban, and the box on which he sat, was a single piece. Before the automaton was an array of numbered cards, and a bell, and his hands were poised in readiness. The face bore a serious expression. I noticed that his generous moustache closely resembled that of his constructor.

'Can he operate from this position?' asked Holmes.

'No, he only does so when he takes the stage,' replied Mr Cooke. 'Poor fellow — he works so hard, and he likes to rest between performances.'

We could see no means to suggest how Psycho was operated by any living hand; in fact, as we looked over the curious machine and his surroundings, our host smiled mischievously, for he could easily guess our purpose. He was kind enough to open the back of the little man, where we could see that his interior was filled with machinery as complex as any chiming clock. The box could not be taken apart, but the width and depth could not have contained any creature able to operate such a device.

'It has been suggested that there are invisible wires or magnets underneath the stage,' said Maskelyne with a laugh. 'People have searched for them in vain. The space does not allow it, and it cannot be safely lit. There is an access door,' he added, pointing to a hatch rather less than a foot square, level with the boards of the backstage platform, which could be lifted by a hinged metal ring. On either side there were small vents in the boards, with thick glass which would provide a glimmer of illumination below when the house lights were on. 'But, as you see, it is very small. It will, however, admit a dog, which enables us to keep the theatre free of vermin, which would be very inconvenient. If major work was to be carried out under the stage, it would be necessary to lift the floorboards.'

As we walked along the rear of the stage, I happened to notice from the little flash of alertness in my friend's eyes that he had seen something of interest. I hoped for a comment or question, but he was silent, and I decided to remain so myself. His glance was resting on the floor at the back of the stage, a place where there was nothing obvious to be seen. I dared not look too closely at it, so as not to draw any attention to the spot. I thought that Maskelyne would be more generous with his time, and more forthcoming if he thought his secrets were safe from us.

The tour done, preparations for the matinee commenced, and Holmes and I were able to enjoy a coffee in a nearby café as we waited for the doors to open for the audience.

'The secret of how Psycho works has been discussed extensively in the newspapers and journals,' said Holmes. 'Importantly, it is well known that the space underneath the stage at the Egyptian Hall is much smaller than that in purpose-built theatres. For this reason, there are no trapdoors in the main stage. This limits ways in which the mechanism can be worked from below. The risk of fire, which is a constant anxiety in all theatres, would render some form of engine prohibitively dangerous. If there were wires and cables connecting it to some source of operative energy which was positioned behind the curtain, the noise would be too apparent. Those people who are invited onto the stage and walk freely around it looking for some connection, have seen nothing obvious. Some people have suggested Psycho is powered by magnetism, but that theory has failed every test. The idea that a child or person of short stature, or even a dog, might be concealed inside it, must surely be dismissed. But what feature makes Psycho different from all other such machines?'

He sipped his coffee. I wondered whether he was hoping for a reply, or if this was simply a rhetorical question. 'It is not like a clockwork machine,' I ventured. 'It has to respond to questions and problems put to it.'

'That is true. But what is unique about its construction?'

'The glass cylinder,' I said. 'I can't recall ever having seen anything like it.'

'I concur,' said Holmes. 'Therefore we must ask ourselves, what is the purpose of that glass? It is thick, strong glass, able to support the weight of the apparatus. Any other construction made of wood or metal might have done the same. So — why glass? On the one hand it demonstrates to the mystified onlooker that there are no levers or pulleys, cables or cords connected to the apparatus. But does it have another purpose? Let us think into the mind of the magician. He shows us the glass, wherein nothing can be concealed; in fact, he makes a great display of it. There is no trick, he is saying to us, the glass column is quite empty, and we are invited to examine it and see this for ourselves. Maybe that absence of anything obvious, that very emptiness, is the whole secret. Our next question is, does the cylinder really contain nothing?'

'Nothing at all,' I said, 'nothing visible, only — wait! Of course! It contains air.'

'Which may be expanded or compressed,' said Holmes. 'I wondered, therefore, might a man lie underneath the stage — if there happens to be some secret access large enough to admit a man, that we have not been shown — with some means of operating Psycho? A small gap in the floorboards would be sufficient. But no. Psycho reacts in such a way that any secret operator must receive both sight and sound from above in order to achieve his miracles. In a game of whist onstage he must be able to view the cards laid down and respond to the play.'

'Does he receive verbal clues from Mr Maskelyne?'

'I have listened carefully, and noticed nothing that could be interpreted in that way.'

'You saw something,' I said. 'At the back of the stage.'

'I did — not precisely something, but the absence of something. There were four little impressions on the surface of the boards, indicating that an item with four legs has rested there. It is just above the little hinged door. And to leave such a mark it must rest in that exact position whenever it is placed there. I was not able to look closely but I think an apparatus must be brought in just before Psycho takes the stage, attached to some device installed underneath the stage, and is then removed and locked away afterwards. Not a machine, but perhaps some kind of bellows which, with care, will not make a sound. That secret lies with only two men: Mr Maskelyne, who is on stage with Psycho, and Mr Cooke, who stands behind the curtain.'

We finished our coffee. Holmes glanced at his pocket watch and rose from his seat. 'Now,' he said, 'let us go and catch our spy.'

CHAPTER TWELVE

Armed with the knowledge gained from our inspection, we returned to the theatre for the matinee. Family parties, mainly mothers, nursemaids and young children were a considerable presence in the auditorium. The sound of youthful chattering was a babble of excitement.

On stage, the wondrous cabinet provided miracles and music as before, but Prince Chandra amused with a variety of tricks that did not involve plunging a sword into his wife, Monsieur Gaston provided colourful illusions with toys, scarves and puppets, the quack doctor confused his foolish victim without removing his head, and Yamadaya was no longer sinister in black, but playful in green and gold. Psycho, however, was not on his best behaviour. He occasionally refused to respond to questions and failed to solve the simplest of sums. The children in the audience squealed in amusement when Maskelyne insinuated that he was being very naughty and ought to go to school and learn his lessons.

The matinee done, the audience filed out, and once the performers and assistants had gone, the theatre was ours. We secured the exits, then Holmes and I mounted the stage and opened the main curtains. The Cabinet of Wonders was in place, and we checked that it was empty and locked. There was no-one lurking in the wings, the internal corridors or the dressing rooms. Tables stood in the wings on either side to be provided with the props needed for the performances, but they were empty. Psycho was standing on his little wooden platform behind the back curtain, the glass cylinder at his side. As far as we were aware, we were alone.

'What now?' I asked as we returned to the auditorium, taking seats in the front row.

'We wait,' said Holmes. 'If we need to take any action I will signal to you. We might have to mount the stage directly, or go up the side corridors to the rear. I will signal thus.' He gestured with his hand to show me what he meant.

'What are we waiting for?' I whispered.

Holmes laid a finger to his lips. 'Listen,' he said softly.

In the silence, it was all too easy to imagine the sound of creeping footfalls, the hushed breath of secret intruders. Holmes remained impassive, but I knew his senses were almost superhumanly alert. Minutes passed, and then I was sure I really had heard something. I glanced at Holmes, and he nodded. He had heard it too. A soft sound, like the scurrying of mice in a nest, and then a slight creak. It was hard to pinpoint where the noise was coming from. It was not in the large space of the auditorium, but possibly backstage or even underneath it. I was reminded of Maskelyne's mention of vermin, and wondered if it was time he employed a terrier. And then we heard a little burst of laughter, and a thrill of excitement moved up my spine.

'Mr Sherlock Holmes,' came a high mocking voice. It undoubtedly emanated from the stage, but we could see no-one there.

'That is my name,' said Holmes calmly. 'May I have yours?'

'Don't you know me?' The voice replied, teasingly. 'You have seen me. I can do many things; I can even talk when I want to. I can tell your fortune. My name is Psycho.'

As it spoke, the back curtains moved apart, as if someone or something was about to pass through them onto the stage. We heard movement — not footsteps, but something sliding across the boards. Gradually, the edge of Psycho's little wooden platform came into view, and eventually we saw the figure of Psycho himself. As ever, its face was without expression.

The curtains fell back into position. Whoever was operating Psycho must have been out of sight behind the Cabinet of Wonders.

I glanced at Holmes to see if he wanted us to act, but he shook his head. 'Not yet,' he whispered. 'Wait for my signal, and then move fast.'

Unruffled, he addressed the figure. 'What is my fortune?' he asked.

'You may rise, but you will fall,' said the high voice. I was relieved to see that the automaton's lips did not move. 'Your fame will be short-lived. Go from here, do not return, and all may still be well.'

'You are a false prophet!' declared Holmes and gave his signal. We rose to our feet and ran, Holmes rushing up the steps to the stage, while I flung myself through a side door. I raced up the stairs, through the door where only staff were usually permitted — which had been left open for us — and found myself backstage, where Psycho had previously stood. Only the glass cylinder rested there. I was alone. I parted the back curtains and joined Holmes on the stage, which was empty apart from the Cabinet of Wonders and Psycho. We inspected the cabinet, but it remained locked. I peered into the little window. No-one was inside.

Holmes again motioned me to remain silent. He walked quietly over to the little access door and stood beside it.

'I think you had better come out, whoever you are,' he said in a loud voice. 'We were expecting you.'

There was a faint shuffling sound from under the stage.

'I mean you no harm,' continued Holmes. 'Let us talk. I would like you to explain yourself. If you have done no wrong, then I promise I will let you go.'

I stared at the tiny door hatch, wondering what kind of individual could be down there.

'We can't go after our intruder,' Holmes said to me. 'And a lantern would be most inadvisable, which is a shame, as I would be most curious to know what device has been installed under the stage. It must have been done during one of the times when the hall was closed for refurbishment.' He lifted the hatch door using the hinged metal ring. 'I know you are in there,' he called down. 'And the exits are closed, so you cannot escape. Come, now.'

We waited a little longer and eventually, after the sound of further movement, a small, tousled head peered out, and a rather dusty little boy, with a face as grey as a ghost, rose from the depths, and stood before us. He was as thin as a sack of bones, and just able to wriggle through the aperture, although I thought that his days of success in that feat were numbered.

'I haven't taken anything, it was just a joke,' he said, defensively.

'And a splendid one it was, too,' said Holmes, cheerily. 'What an intrepid fellow you are. But I think you had better not do it again. I have been told that there may be rats nesting under there, and the owners send a dog down to kill them. Now, you have a choice: you can explain everything to me, or I can bring you before Mr Maskelyne, who may not be so forgiving.'

I rather thought Maskelyne was a forgiving man, especially for a childish prank, but it suited Holmes to allow the boy to think otherwise.

The boy sniffed and rubbed his nose. 'All right, I'll talk,' he said.

'Then let us make ourselves comfortable,' said Holmes, still in friendly fashion, and we went to sit on the front row of the auditorium, with our charge placed between us in case he should be tempted to run away.

'First,' said Holmes, 'I would like to know your name.'

I was expecting to hear the boy admit to 'Jack Smith' or 'John Brown' — the usual claim made by a miscreant in order to conceal his true identity, but instead he gave us a surly look and said, 'Orlando Fishwick.'

'Ah,' said Holmes. 'Then you must be the son of Oliver Fishwick, better known as Mr Fiz, who presented Osric to the world? I assume you must have assisted him with that?'

'Yes, but he doesn't do that anymore, since we got into trouble; and in any case, it's broken.'

'How old are you?'

The boy straightened his shoulders and stretched a little taller. 'I'm almost nine.'

'And your mother? Is she part of these theatrical endeavours?'

Orlando shook his head. 'No. I've not seen her in a while. It's just me and Father and my sister, Jessica.'

'So, to business,' said Holmes, still friendly but in a rather more serious tone. 'What were you doing here and who sent you?'

'Mr Ashbury sent me,' said the boy. 'He's Father's manager. He told me your name, Mr Holmes. He's seen you about here; said you were getting too interested in what was going on at the hall. He wanted to give you a warning. He told me what to say. I don't know what he meant by it.'

'I think I can guess,' said Holmes gravely. 'I have been given warnings before. I do not fear them. And what has been your mission here? To explore backstage and discover the secrets of Psycho? I think a great many people would like to know them.'

'Yes, I can get under the stage, but it's hard to see much down there, and I didn't like to strike a match. All I can see is a big tube. When Psycho is working, they lift up the door and something happens behind the curtains. I don't know why, but if I squeeze or bend the tube while Psycho is on stage, it doesn't work properly.'

'Even if Mr Ashbury could find out how Psycho is operated,' I said, 'I doubt he could make one of his own. No-one really knows how it works, other than Mr Maskelyne.'

'And I assume,' said Holmes, 'that when you play your tricks you enter the theatre with a ticket like the others? And leave with them afterwards?'

'Yes.'

'How did you know about the door into the space under the stage?'

'That was easy. They invite children up on the stage to see Psycho after it does its act. Mr Ashbury told me that I should look about for trapdoors and hiding places. There aren't any trapdoors on the main stage, but I went behind the cabinet to see if there was anything hidden there, and when I looked through the back curtains there it was. But the old man, the one who died, he was there and saw me and told me to get back on stage.'

'How were you able to hide and then leave without anyone seeing you?'

'I couldn't while the old man was on the lookout, but after he died I thought I had a chance; the younger man wasn't so sharp, you see. I just had to pick the right time and move quick.'

'What does your father do now?' asked Holmes. 'Is he still managed by Mr Ashbury?'

'Yes — he talks to the spirits,' said Orlando. 'And they talk back. He makes ghosts appear. He has a cabinet — not like the one here — it's a room where the ghosts come out from behind a curtain. Then they go back inside and when he draws the curtain, people see they have gone.'

'Is your father's stage name Prospero?' I asked. 'I have seen him advertised in the newspapers. If he attracts the attention of Mr Maskelyne, he might be advised to go elsewhere.'

'Well, he can't. Ashbury keeps his people under his thumb. We all stay in the same house.'

'There are others?' queried Holmes.

'There is Monsieur Bonfleur. He makes flowers and butterflies appear out of nothing. Then he throws a silk shawl over his wife, and she disappears.'

'Does Mr Ashbury do any conjuring himself?'

'No, or at least I have never seen him do any.'

'Well, you tell him from me,' said Holmes, 'that I like to enquire into mysteries and find out the truths that people like to conceal. I am not afraid of him and will not cease my endeavours.'

'I hope he is not a cruel master,' I said.

'Well, it don't do to say no to him,' said the boy. 'Jessica doesn't like him at all. She says he smells funny, and once he said something rude to her and she stamped on his foot. But he did promise she can be a lady assistant to a magician when she is older.'

'How old is your sister?' asked Holmes.

'Eleven.'

'I am pleased that she has a father and brother to take good care of her,' said Holmes. He took a card from his pocket. 'If you should happen to need any assistance, I can be contacted here.' He glanced at me, and I provided my card. 'You should let your father know that you have spoken to me today. If he has anything to tell me, I will be glad to listen.'

We secured the auditorium and escorted the boy from the premises, then we went to make our report to Mr Maskelyne, hoping he would greet our findings as good news.

Mr Cooke kindly retrieved his tireless partner from his private workshop, and we all proceeded to the stage to talk. 'You should have no further trouble with Psycho,' said Holmes. 'As you can see, the device has been moved from its usual position, but I do not believe any more than that was done. The intruder was Orlando Fishwick, who is small enough to pass through the access door and get underneath the stage. From there he was able to interfere with the machine's operation. I have given him a warning and I doubt he will try it again, but until he has grown a little more, I suggest you make the aperture narrower.'

Maskelyne frowned, and he and Cooke hurried to make an external examination of Psycho. 'We will have to carry out some tests before the evening performance,' he said, 'but it appears undamaged. I doubt the child did this on his own account. Did his father put him up to it?'

'It was Mr Ashbury, who manages his father. Mr Fishwick is now operating as a medium under the name of Prospero.'

'I am grateful to you, gentlemen,' said Maskelyne. 'Please continue your vigilance. You may have tickets gratis any time you wish.'

'Do you intend to expose Mr Fishwick as a fraud?' I asked.

Maskelyne sighed. 'No, he has troubles enough and there are two children to support. No man who relied upon Mr Ashbury has ever profited from that arrangement, and there are many who have lived to regret it.'

CHAPTER THIRTEEN

I was obliged to devote the next few days almost entirely to my studies, since the spectre of my final examinations later that year was looming ever closer. My intention, assuming I was to qualify, was eventually to acquire my own medical practice, but before I could do so, I would be employed for two more years at Barts as a junior surgeon. My hours would then be far more regulated than they had been as a student. I had been gaining a wealth of practical experience in assisting Holmes, but I was concerned that he would be unable to appreciate the additional demands of my medical career. I also feared that whenever he urgently required my presence, I would find it hard to deny him.

I was in the students' library, musing on this dilemma, when the door opened and Holmes peered in. He said nothing, conversation in that place being discouraged, but his look told me all I needed to know. I put my books away and joined him in the corridor.

'Inspector Knight is here to speak to us,' he said. 'There is a lecture room free.'

The inspector was undoubtedly unused to involving youthful consultants with no relevant qualifications, but as we arrived for our meeting, I thought his attitude towards us was considerably easier than at our prior encounter.

'I have taken the opportunity, Mr Holmes, of speaking to your professor here,' said Knight. 'He spoke very highly of your work in examining the scene of the murder in the great auk case, and the evidence you secured. Sergeant Lestrade has also praised the assistance you have given to the police on several occasions. You are not, I take it, a professional detective?'

'Not yet,' said Holmes. 'I do not ask to be remunerated for my work.'

'I have learned from Mr Maskelyne that he and Mr Cooke have decided to employ you both as private investigators,' said Knight. He took a deep breath. 'Now that is their business, of course, but I do not wish you to be cajoled into assuming that they cannot therefore be involved in the death of Mr Tapper. It is very probable that Mr Tapper met his end while Mr Maskelyne was in the building. The only witness to Mr Cooke's location that evening is his wife, and she cannot be precise as to the time he came home. Either man might have had the opportunity to tie up Mr Tapper to extract information from him if they thought he might be in the pay of spies. Mr Maskelyne in particular is not a man one wishes to cross.'

'I must agree with your evaluation,' said Holmes, 'although thus far, Mr Maskelyne's dealings with opposition and charlatans have always remained within the law.'

Knight nodded in acknowledgement. 'We do know that Mr Tapper did not appear at his usual haunt, the King George Tavern, on the night in question, so he must have remained in the hall between ten o'clock and his death.'

'I am afraid we have not been able to learn a great deal about Mr Tapper,' continued Holmes.

'He has been a hard man to learn about,' said Knight. 'I have spoken to Mr and Mrs Fergus, but they have almost nothing to say about him. It does not appear that he made any enemies in London, either while working at the Egyptian Hall or at Crystal Palace. He did his work and spent his evenings in the public house with his beer and a game of cards. He neither owed money nor lent it. The only items of note in his property were some handbills, the kind theatres give out in the street. He was occupied sometimes in distributing these outside the theatres, or in hostelries, and must have kept a few as mementoes. The majority are for London theatres, though there are also a few in Liverpool, where it appears he lived and worked for some years before he came to London.'

'May I see them?' asked Holmes.

'I thought you might wish to,' said Knight. He produced an envelope from his pocket and passed it to Holmes, who carried it to the lecturer's table. There, he extracted a bundle of handbills, and laid them out to examine them.

'I have notified the police in Liverpool, and they have been conducting enquiries on my behalf,' Knight continued, 'but they have yet to discover a record of Mr Tapper ever being arrested or questioned in connection with any crime. The Liverpool theatres are mainly varieties, and it is confirmed that he was employed there for some years as a stagehand. Tapper did briefly work for the magician known as the Wizard of the North before he departed on a world tour in the autumn of 1870. Mr Tapper did not accompany him, but the experience and recommendation enabled him to find work in London. I can't rule out the possibility that Tapper made enemies which prompted him to leave Liverpool. He might have had debts there we know nothing of. Or perhaps he discovered something which placed him in danger and that has caught up with him. We don't know if he ever married or had a family to support. He told Fergus he didn't, but he might not have been truthful. Perhaps he did marry and left Liverpool to escape his responsibilities. Enquiries are being made.'

I was at Holmes's side, surveying the assortment of handbills. 'These notices give the days and month but not the year,' I said, studying the gaudily printed papers.

'The theatres concerned have confirmed that they relate to the period from 1866 to 1871,' said Knight.

Holmes had been reading the handbills without noticeable appreciation of their content. 'Apart from ballet and opera, which I fear in such places are most imperfectly rendered, they promise grotesque dancers, comic vocalists, a troupe of performing goats, a French Herculean lady, a man with a magic barrel and another who plays ten tambourines at once,' he said. 'What a wealth of wonders we have here!'

'And who knows what their real names were?' said Knight. 'Some of the acts just make up something fancy or copy the names of better-known performers. There's even a performing monkey called Blondin, who I am quite sure is a perfect marvel on the tightrope. But as I said, enquiries continue and I am hoping the theatre managers might have something to suggest.'

I sensed that Holmes was content to leave that part of the investigation to the Liverpool police. 'I assume I am not permitted to take these away for further study,' he said.

'I am sorry, Mr Holmes, the Chief Inspector would be very unhappy with me if I allowed potential evidence to leave the possession of the police.'

Holmes accepted the situation without protest and made some jottings in his little notebook.

'Do you have anything to add, Mr Holmes?'

'Not as yet, but if I learn anything of value I will let you know, and I hope you will return the favour.'

Knight gathered up the handbills, and the meeting ended on a cordial basis.

'It seems as though the answer might lie in Liverpool,' I said, after the inspector had left.

'Perhaps,' replied Holmes. 'I do have one line of enquiry to pursue, but it would not be wise to make any assumptions or share my thoughts with the inspector until I have checked the facts.'

'What is that?'

'One of the performers on the bill of the Star Playhouse. Liverpool's favourite songstress — Miss Selina Good, the girl with the golden voice. That may or may not reward some enquiry.'

It took me a moment or two to understand his suggestion. 'You think she might be Mrs Selina Goodgold?'

'Possibly.'

'That was her stage name, perhaps.'

'Yes, but if it is she, it is a coincidence, is it not, that she used such a name *before* she met her husband. A small point, I know, but it irks me. I have also noted the names of the conjurors mentioned on some of the handbills. If there are any interesting tales to be told, I am in the right place to hear them.'

'Scandal and gossip?' I asked.

'Yes, and a careful sifting of the truth from the lies.'

CHAPTER FOURTEEN

We sought out Mr Maskelyne at the theatre but were told he was in his workshop and not to be disturbed unless in an emergency. Mr Cooke, however, obligingly agreed to speak to us.

Holmes read out the names of the conjurors he had noted from the handbills, and I saw from Cooke's expression — his smiles, frowns and emphatic nods — that they were all familiar to him.

'Yes, the Wizard of the North, Professor Anderson. He too exposed the trickery of the Davenport brothers and was most celebrated in his day. His performance of the bullet catch, which he did impeccably, brought him considerable fame. But he was known for being quarrelsome and lost as many fortunes as he made. Tapper mentioned having worked for him. I think it was a source of some pride.'

'Did Anderson quarrel with Tapper?'

'I can't say. But the Wizard is gone now, he died about four years ago. Then there is Herrmann the Great. He performed here very successfully some years ago. He is currently abroad, touring America I believe. And Baron Hartwig Seeman — I had heard he was in India, trying to acquire the secrets of the street magicians.'

'What about Dr Peralta?' asked Holmes.

'Ah, yes.' A sorrowful expression passed over Cooke's normally cheery features, and the long drooping side whiskers gave him the appearance of a melancholy bloodhound. 'That was a sad business.'

'Oh?' Holmes paused. 'I saw something in the press, some weeks ago, concerning the death of a conjuror. Was that he?'

'It was indeed. His real name was Potter, but he thought that too commonplace for a magician, so on stage he was Dr Peralta. He was never — I suppose I can say it now — of the top rank, and as a result suffered greatly from despondency at his lack of recognition. He also drank to excess, and this took its toll. His hands often trembled, and he arrived on stage the worse for that indulgence too many times and was unable to perform. Eventually no-one would give him work. He was reduced to begging in the street, performing simple tricks for pennies. Peralta was found dead in his lodgings a few weeks ago. The inquest recorded his death as a suicide.'

'Did he know Tapper?'

'If he did, I don't know about it. Tapper never mentioned him. There was one thing, though. You said that Tapper was supposed to know a secret he was using to extort money from somebody. Peralta also used to say he knew a secret. Whether it was the same one Tapper knew or something else entirely, I couldn't say. It might have been all in his imagination. He used to mumble to himself that he had information which he could sell to the right person for a good price, if he chose. But he was so often inebriated that no-one took any notice.'

'Perhaps there was something in it,' said Holmes. 'Is there someone who knew him and might speak to me?'

'I think Peralta was once managed by Mr Ashbury, who is in London now, promoting his new find, Prospero the Mystic, and another magician, Bonfleur. Perhaps Peralta's secret, whatever it was, related to Ashbury, who was always underhand in his methods. But if Tapper learned about it and tried to blackmail Ashbury, I don't think he would have got very far. Ashbury has been sued any number of times, but he always seems to wriggle his way out of the consequences.'

'I have a request, Mr Cooke,' said Holmes. 'I would like to speak to Mrs Goodgold, as there were some questions I omitted to ask when I last spoke to her. It concerns her career on the stage, prior to her marriage. Is it possible to speak to her in confidence?'

'I will have a word with her now,' said Cooke.

Fortunately, the private interview was easily arranged as the lady was sitting in the wings of the small upstairs stage, busy mending some costumes. Her husband was ensconced in the space that served them as a dressing room, writing a piece for a future performance, an activity in which he preferred not to be disturbed.

'Mrs Goodgold, I thank you for allowing us a few minutes of your time,' said Holmes. 'I wish to ask about a small matter to complete my enquiries.'

'It is no trouble at all,' she said, brightly, her busy needle never pausing in its work.

'It relates to your earlier stage career. Have you ever appeared professionally at the Liverpool Star Playhouse?'

She was surprised but not concerned by this question. 'Why, yes, I have. I did a short season there some years ago.'

'This was before you were married?'

'Yes, it was.'

'In fact, it was before you met your husband?'

'Yes.'

'When did you meet Mr Goodgold?'

'We were married in April 1874, and we had then known each other for a year. But why do you want to know about Liverpool?'

'I ask because some handbills have been found amongst the late Mr Tapper's possessions relating to that theatre, and it has been confirmed that he worked there for a time.'

'Ah, I understand you now, and you would like me to say whether I recall meeting Mr Tapper?'

'If you wouldn't mind.'

Mrs Goodgold paused in her sewing and appeared to be giving the matter some thought, but finally shook her head and resumed stitching. 'No, I really don't remember him. But I presume he was working backstage, not as a performer. My set was a very simple one. There was a backdrop which resembled a cottage garden, and a few urns with little trees and flowering shrubs. Just painted on wood, of course, but all very dainty. I used to sing about the delights of a garden; roses, birds, honeybees, butterflies. There were some men who worked for the theatre and prepared the scenery and arranged the set, but I really recall nothing about them.'

'You were billed as Miss Selina Good?'

'Yes, I was.'

'The girl with the golden voice?'

She hesitated, and I am sure she began to perceive Holmes's next question. 'Yes, such elegant praise. I did not write that myself.'

'If I might venture to say so,' Holmes continued,' I was struck by the similarity of your name at that time, with your married surname, which you did not acquire until several years later. As you have said, you did not even know Mr Goodgold then. It seems to be too much of a coincidence. I know many people do perform under a name not their own. Was your husband's name always Goodgold when he took the stage?'

She gave a cheery little laugh. 'Oh, no. I must take you into my confidence now as you have found out a secret. How clever you are! My dear husband was born Jack Huggins. I think you would agree that that is not really a suitable name for a performer of serious theatrical recitations, as he was then. He was advertised on playbills as "Signor Hugin, Dramatic Personations, the man with a thousand voices". When we married and devised our new act, we took the name Goodgold. And yes, it was a play on the words of my former billing. I thought it sounded rather well, and people remember it.'

'I think,' said Holmes, who was not smiling, 'in view of the fact that your husband chose to omit these details, I will be obliged to ask him once more if he can recall ever having previously met Mr Tapper. Either as Goodgold, Huggins or Hugin.'

'I am quite sure he has not,' she replied. 'On the few occasions when we saw the man here, Jonathan did not mention he knew him, and neither engaged him in conversation nor tried to avoid him. But let me talk to my husband, once he has completed his work, and if he has anything more to tell you which would assist your enquiries, I will urge him to speak to you.'

We thanked her, and left her to her sewing, although I noticed as we departed that she did not ply her needle, but sat thoughtfully with her hands in her lap.

'Do you think Mr Goodgold has anything further to tell us?' I asked Holmes.

'I do,' said Holmes, 'and we shall not have long to wait.'

CHAPTER FIFTEEN

During those early years when Holmes was acquiring the skills and knowledge that he required for his chosen profession, his cramped and overstuffed rooms in Montague Street rapidly became unsuitable for the purpose of conducting interviews and, to my mind, something of a disgrace. I did not say it to him openly, but I am sure from my expression whenever I visited him and looked about the place that he realised and understood my opinion on the matter. He was not by nature a man who accumulated items purely for decorative or monetary value, which was a blessing, otherwise there would have been no space for the occupant. Everything he collected had a purpose, a meaning, but since his work as a detective demanded expertise and information on an extraordinary variety of subjects, the sheer volume of the material which grew by the day left little room for the daily life of the tenant.

It was obvious that he required a larger set of rooms, but without prying into his affairs, I gathered that his purse would not allow it. For the moment, as he was able to conduct his chemistry experiments during his course work at Barts, he did not need to set up a laboratory in his home, but I feared what might happen when his course work was done. There was an unspoken understanding that Holmes and I would never agree to combine our resources and share a larger apartment. Much as I admire Holmes, have been his loyal companion on many an adventure, and remain to this day his firm friend, we could never have lived together. The clutter, the pervading stench of tobacco, and his indifferent mastery of the violin would have been intolerable to me.

This did mean that as Holmes's involvement in detective work increased, and he required a private location to conduct interviews, especially one which would not have repelled anyone with delicate nostrils, he shamelessly commandeered my tidy little parlour. I often found myself clearing my table of books at very little notice and had to be prepared to take on the duty of a mere secretary in my own home.

Thus it was that a matter of hours after our conversation with Mrs Goodgold, I received a terse note from Holmes to the effect that Mr Jonathan Goodgold had requested an interview, and Holmes had agreed to see him at my rooms on the condition that he did not bring his cat.

I made a note of the time, rearranged my schedule of work, and ensured that tea would be provided. Tea is a stimulant to the brain, its comforting familiarity encouraging conversation and refreshing the throat of the speaker should it become dry or choked with emotion.

'Mr Holmes, Mr Stamford,' said Jonathan Goodgold, as he joined us. 'I am very grateful for the opportunity to speak to you privately.'

'I welcome this discussion,' said Holmes. 'But you must undertake to tell me all you know and speak only the truth. I feel that Archie might not always have been entirely open with me during our previous conversation. He took it upon himself to answer those questions which you wished to avoid.'

Mr Goodgold smiled with just a hint of embarrassment. 'I have been told that you enjoy the reputation of being a man from whom it is hard to keep secrets,' he said, 'and therefore I feel it is better to be quite plain with you.'

'Please proceed.'

'Before I speak further,' said Mr Goodgold, as I poured the tea, 'I wish to make it very clear that neither I nor my dear wife had anything to do with the death of Mr Tapper.'

Holmes merely inclined his head to acknowledge that he understood what he was being told, but his expression did not reveal any judgement.

'You should know,' Goodgold continued, 'that I was not always employed as I am now. My earlier career was as a conjuror and illusionist, in which I enjoyed some moderate success. My stage name, which I then used, was Tourmalin. I appeared in a number of towns in both England and Scotland, although I never toured abroad. About eight years ago I found that I had a rival whose performance bore some similarities to mine. I have never copied another man, but I did sometimes wonder if he had copied me. I could never prove it of course. His name was Dr Peralta.'

I immediately recalled that this was the conjuror who had recently expired in unfortunate circumstances. I glanced at Holmes, whose features gave nothing away. Neither of us wished to interrupt our guest.

'I never met the man,' said Goodgold, 'in fact, I had the impression that he was avoiding me in case I took issue with him. When I spoke to managements, I discovered that he or his promoter had been making enquiries about where I was due to perform next. He would then book a theatre in that town for the week before me and advertise his performances with handbills and posters, so that when I came, my audiences were diminished. I often lost bookings entirely for this reason. There was nothing I could do to prevent it, and I would never stoop to any act of revenge. It is not in my nature. I decided instead to challenge him by devising a new spectacle for my repertoire, one that would attract the attention of the public, and was something that he had never performed. I decided — and Heaven help me, how I wish I had not — to perform the bullet catch.'

Goodgold took a deep breath. 'Have either of you ever seen the bullet catch performed?'

We both admitted we had not. 'I have been told it is accompanied by considerable risks. Mr Maskelyne will not entertain it,' said Holmes.

'There are many different methods of performing it,' said our visitor, 'many variations on the effect one desires to achieve, but one aspect never changes. The most important feature for the man who undertakes the bullet catch, is the meticulous preparation of every item used each time it is performed, without fail. On stage, it should never be hurried. Time is needed to engage the audience, arouse their anticipation and to demonstrate the extreme dangers of the proceeding. Of course, correctly performed, there should be no danger at all, but as all conjurors know, there have been exceptions when precautions were not properly taken, or there was some small variation in procedure. I have read of De Grisy, who accidentally caused the death of his own son when attempting to portray the drama of William Tell, and went mad as a consequence. And there have been others, such as Herr Blume, who was shot with his own gun. I had successfully performed the bullet catch many times before —' and here Goodgold closed his eyes as if experiencing a stab of pain — 'before the terrible tragedy occurred.'

There was a significant pause as we all sipped our tea. Mr Goodgold was rather thirstier than Holmes and I.

Holmes broke the silence. 'I would be grateful if you could describe in detail the act as you performed it.'

Goodgold nodded. 'I will, but on the strict understanding that I cannot divulge my secrets, which are the most precious commodity any conjuror may have.'

'Then explain how it would appear to the audience.'

'Very well.' Goodgold put his cup down and clasped his hands together. 'Imagine, if you will, that you are watching me as Tourmalin, on stage. The materials I use are very simple: a pistol, a box of bullets, a flask of gunpowder, a ramrod, wadding, a metal dish, a target, and a china plate. I call up at least two volunteers from the audience to see that all is done fairly. First, I set up the target to one side of the stage. I will have already warned the stagehands and other performers that they must not stand in the wings on that side. I set the plate in front of the target supported on a wooden stand. I invite the volunteers to examine the pistol, bullets, ramrod and wadding. Often, some of those who volunteer will be familiar with firearms, and it is important to receive their approval. I then sprinkle a little gunpowder onto the metal dish and put a flame to it to show that it is genuine. Also, it produces a very pleasant visual effect. And then to charge the pistol. Slowly, carefully, deliberately. Every movement I make is visible. Nothing is concealed. Powder first, then wadding, using the ramrod. I ask a volunteer to select at random a bullet from the box, and he hands it to me. I hold it up so the audience can see it.' Goodgold suited the action to the word, lifting one hand as if an imaginary bullet was clasped delicately between the tips of thumb and forefinger. 'And then, I place it in the barrel of the pistol, asking the volunteer to use another piece of wadding and the ramrod. Finally, I fit the percussion cap. I next demonstrate that the pistol and bullet are real. Warning the volunteers to stand well back, I take aim and fire at the target. The shot passes through the plate, breaking it, and buries itself safely in the target. A volunteer then examines the target and confirms that the bullet is there. The audience now knows, or believes, that both the gun and its ammunition are genuine. The danger is genuine.'

Holmes nodded but made no comment.

'And now to the trick,' Goodgold continued. 'I tell the audience that the next time the gun is fired it will be pointed at me, and I will endeavour to catch the bullet in my teeth. At this point, I hear the audience utter a little gasp of fear and anticipation. I ask one of the volunteers to select the next bullet from the box. This is the one to be used in the trick. This time I do not handle the bullet myself. I merely hold the pistol while he loads it as before. I ask the volunteer if he is willing to fire the pistol at me. Some men are nervous of it and decline, in which case I politely ask him to step down and request another volunteer. Others are willing to do so.

'Now comes the pinnacle of the illusion. My exposure to deadly danger by standing in front of the target holding before my face another china plate. I myself am now the main target. I tell the audience that when the gun is fired the bullet will pass through the plate, breaking it, and I will catch it in my teeth.

'The volunteer is by now very nervous, so I reassure him, saying that he must take careful aim, pointing at the plate which is held in front of my mouth. He raises the pistol. His aim is poor, but for the trick to work that is of no consequence. The sense of apprehension in the audience is now at its height. No-one watching this dares to breathe. Some even cover their faces. He pulls the trigger. The gun fires. The plate shatters. I do not fall but show the audience the bullet which I have caught in my mouth — there it is held between my teeth! The relief is immeasurable. That is the illusion. I thank the volunteer and accept the plaudits of the audience.'

Goodgold paused, his features contorted by strain. We allowed him a little time to recover. I poured more tea, and he refreshed himself gratefully.

'What happened on the fateful occasion?' asked Holmes, softly.

Our visitor took a deep breath, gathering his nerves. 'I was performing in Bristol at the time. It all began as before. The man who loaded the gun declined to fire it and returned to his seat. Another gentleman stepped forward. Earnest, trusting. I heard later that he was thirty years of age, an architect, married with three young children. His name was Percival Winstone. He agreed to fire the pistol, and I handed it to him. I took up the position and he fired.' Goodgold's voice broke a little, but he forced himself to continue. 'The gun exploded in his hand. One piece struck him in the neck and severed a blood vessel. There was a doctor in the audience who rushed to his aid, but there was nothing anyone could do for him. The poor fellow died on the stage in a pool of blood. To add to the horror, his wife was in the audience. I am only thankful the children were not there to see it.'

'Were any of the volunteers known to you previously?' asked Holmes.

'No. There are conjurors who sometimes employ accomplices in the audience — I will not reveal who they are and for what purpose — but that was not necessary in my performance.'

'Did the china plate shatter?'

'Yes, it did. It is supposed to do so as part of the illusion. The enquiry into the death made nothing of that point and assumed that it had been struck by a flying fragment.'

'You already had a bullet concealed in your mouth?'

He gave a pained smile. 'You cannot imagine I really do catch a missile?'

'No, of course not. Was the enquiry able to discover what caused the accident?'

'No. The pistol had been in perfect order. I never failed to check and thoroughly clean it myself before every performance and, of course, it had already been shown to work. The committee of enquiry examined the pieces and also the box of bullets from which the two that had been fired had been selected. It was a box of a dozen, and ten remained. The first one had been extracted from the target. Of the one that had been in the gun when it exploded, and the wadding, nothing remained that could be examined. The conclusion was that I must have made an error in the materials and was at fault.'

'I must assume,' said Holmes, 'that while the bullet fired by you was genuine, the others were not. Were these trick bullets purchased by you? Was the supplier or manufacturer not held to be at fault?'

'They were purchased by me, but I modified the contents by adding something to produce a smoke effect. My sister, who assisted me, was quite sure that there had been no fault, no variation.'

'I see.'

'I could only assume that I had been negligent in some way and admitted responsibility. I was charged with manslaughter, for which I was tried, but was found guilty of a lesser charge and endured a prison sentence. As you can imagine, I did not return to conjuring. The name Tourmalin is forever lost. I took such humble employments as were open to me, working under my real name, which is Huggins, assisting in theatres backstage. I then devised a series of readings from classical literature, which enjoyed some small success. That was how I met my dear wife Selina, who was performing as a songstress. Before proposing marriage, I confessed all to her, and she did not refuse me. It was at her suggestion that we began to perform our entertainment in partnership — the comedy sketches, the recitations, songs and so on.'

'Mr Tapper was not there on the night of the tragedy?'

'No, I am sure of that, or he would have told me. But he had once seen me at another venue, as Tourmalin, performing the bullet catch. When I was engaged at the Egyptian Hall, he recognised me, and I was obliged to pay him for his silence.'

'Does Mrs Goodgold know this?'

'She did not at the time. She does now.'

'Blackmailers, once they fasten their hooks into a victim, seldom let go,' Holmes observed.

'I was aware of the danger,' said Goodgold, 'but we are due to go on tour after my season here and I hoped that Mr Tapper would not be able to threaten me further after I left London. I assure you that I was in no way responsible for his death.'

'My advice to you, Mr Goodgold,' said Holmes, 'is to tell the police your story before they discover it for themselves, in which case they will wonder why you have concealed it.'

'Of course, yes; I know I should have done so,' said Goodgold with a sigh. 'I promise you I will make a full statement to the inspector tomorrow.'

'Do you still practise your conjuring?' asked Holmes.

'I — yes, it is as well not to let those skills die. I do so to keep my fingers flexible, and who knows? One day I might incorporate some simple card or coin tricks into my act.'

'I would appreciate some lessons in the art,' said Holmes.

Goodgold smiled. 'Of course, I would be glad to show you some of the more popular tricks that can be easily acquired.

But the art is perfected not by lessons, but many hours of diligent practice. Do you wish to enter the profession?'

'No, but one never knows when such a skill can be of use.'

Once Goodgold had left us — a far happier man for having unburdened himself — I turned to Holmes. 'Card tricks?' I asked.

'I intend to seek an appointment to speak to Mr Ashbury,' he said. 'He is a devious fellow, and I doubt I would be granted an interview in the usual way or be told the truth if I was. But we have never met face to face. If I was able to represent myself as a conjuror looking for a manager, I might learn something of his methods. And I would very much like to know what secret the late Dr Peralta was concealing.'

CHAPTER SIXTEEN

Holmes, who never did anything by halves, plunged at once into practising the manipulation of playing cards, every spare moment at his disposal being devoted to this study. He also took good advantage of Mr Maskelyne's offer of free tickets. While keeping a watchful eye for any possible suspicious circumstances at the Egyptian Hall, I realised he also particularly wanted to study conjurors for their stage presentation techniques. After spending long hours with my books and in the dissection room, I was happy to accompany him to the theatre on occasion as a brief diversion for my weary mind.

It was during a short break in one such performance to reset the stage that Mr Chandler, who was not yet costumed as Prince Chandra, came to see us. He was in a state of some distraction.

'Mr Stamford, I understand you are a medical man?' he asked. I was about to say that I was as yet a student but would help in any way I could, but he hurried on. 'It is my dear wife, she is very unwell, and I fear she may not be able to perform this evening!'

'Let me see her,' I said, and left my seat to accompany him backstage. Holmes, who always tried to avoid dealing with female afflictions, remained where he was.

There was a small storage space the Chandlers used as a dressing room which was very tidily arranged. It contained all the costumes and properties required for their performance and there was a small shelf with a mirror, brushes and greasepaints. Mrs Chandler, enveloped in a silk wrap, was sitting in the only chair, holding her abdomen, her skin flushed and damp, and looking queasily uncomfortable. I questioned her as to her symptoms and elicited the information that she had recently eaten a savoury pie, which she thought might have disagreed with her. Mr Chandler, who was perfectly well, had been content with a sandwich and had eaten none of the pie. The further symptoms of her disorder confirmed a diagnosis of food poisoning, and it was obvious that it would be unwise in the extreme for her to take the stage.

I was able to reassure them both that it appeared to be a mild case, and as long as Mrs Chandler rested and drank plenty of liquids then it was probable that the upsetting symptoms would soon abate, and she would be able to take the stage again on the following night. I suggested she try a herbal tisane, made with freshly boiled water, the makings of which were on sale in a nearby emporium.

Mr Chandler was relieved that it was nothing worse and went at once to obtain the comforting herbs I had prescribed, but both were upset that Princess Yasmin would not be able to appear.

'I might have asked Mr Cooke to take my wife's place in the basket as he is not a tall man, but he is heavily engaged in taking on some of the duties of the late Mr Tapper,' said Chandler. 'In any case, he has rather obvious whiskers. I don't want to omit the Indian basket trick; that is the high point of the act. It is advertised on all the posters and in the newspapers and everyone expects to see it.' He was contemplating how to perform his act without assistance, when I suddenly saw that he was staring at me in a very odd manner. 'Mr Stamford, excuse me, but I perceive that you are the same stature as my wife, and moreover of a slender figure and without whiskers. I am sure you would fit inside the basket very well.'

I could deny none of this, although I could not see how the presence or absence of whiskers was of any moment.

'Yes!' exclaimed Chandler. 'Please, I beg of you, do assist me. It would not take long for me to show you what to do, it is simplicity itself. And Princess Yasmin's costume, being of a flowing nature would drape very well over your small clothes. There is a headdress with a veil so only your eyes would be seen.'

'You want me to personate Princess Yasmin?' I exclaimed.

He began to estimate my proportions. 'Of course, the audience might notice the difference. You are broader across the shoulders...'

'I should think they would!'

'I know! You will be her sister, Princess Fatima.'

'But I don't know the trick and you are due to appear on stage in just a few minutes!' I protested.

'That would not be a difficulty, I am sure,' said Chandler. 'I will have a quick word with Mr Maskelyne to explain the situation. This is not the first time such a thing has occurred. We ought to be able to change the order of the programme for the last hour so you will have ample time to learn your part.'

It did seem churlish to deny him, and Mrs Chandler begged me very prettily to agree, so I had no option but to do so. The matter was settled quickly, and while Mrs Chandler was dispatched back to their lodgings in a carriage, her husband showed me how to act as a conjuror's assistant. I was obliged to remove my outer garments to be fitted with the costume and submit to the application of greasepaint. The transformation, which I was able to view in the mirror, was quite startling. I have never appeared on stage and admit that I was extremely nervous at the prospect, mainly because I feared I might forget everything I was supposed to do and ruin the performance. While I waited to be called, I tried to distract myself by reading a newspaper which lay in the room. I was hoping for something in the way of entertainment, but it was a daily London paper, folded open at a page regarding the pronouncements of the India Council at Whitehall. It was understandable that the Chandlers would take a close interest in the governance of that country, but it was not the light reading I had hoped for.

Prince Chandra and Princess Fatima were the final act of the evening. I am not at all sure how well I did, but since much of it was handing Prince Chandra the props for the next trick in the correct order and twirling gaily about the stage in distracting draperies, I thought I performed rather well. I was comfortably able to fit myself into the wicker basket, and due to its unusual construction, I left it unnoticed before the sword was thrust into it. The cries of anguish I uttered while lying behind the basket and the appearance of bloodstains on the sword from a receptacle secreted inside it, provided the rest of the illusion. Had the stage been provided with a trapdoor I would have been able to disappear below the boards, but since it was not, I was obliged to leave the stage by crawling underneath the back curtain, while the basket concealed me from view. I then made my way along the side corridors to reappear at the rear of the hall. As I walked towards the stage, waving to the audience, the face veil which was not a precise fit, slipped a little, and there were several gentlemen who gave me a rather interested look, impelling me to hurry onto the stage for the applause.

'I am so very grateful to you,' said Mr Chandler, as we returned to the little dressing room with the properties. 'But I must now return to my lodgings to see my wife.'

'Of course,' I said. 'I will make sure all is left tidy here before I leave.' He uttered a great sigh of relief and hurried away.

I had just unfolded my outer garments from where I had laid them aside and shaken out a few creases prior to getting changed out of my colourful robes, when I heard the door open behind me. I assumed that it might be Chandler returning, having forgotten something, or one of the other acts in the theatre, but then I heard a wheezing sound. I turned around.

In the doorway stood a man I had never seen before, but I knew at once who he must be.

Mr Ashbury entered the room and shut the door behind him. He was a heavily-built man of medium height, with unkempt greying hair and beard, both worn long. His clothing, a thick brown suit and waistcoat, gave off the odour of something worn every day and never cleaned. An old felt hat with a wide brim and a cockade of crumpled feathers in the band, was jammed tightly on his head. A Tyrolean hat, I realised. He moved slowly, leaning on a stout stick. He clearly suffered from some affliction of the chest, but I could not judge what it might be. I was not about to offer him an examination.

'Well now,' he said, 'Mr Stamford, Mr Sherlock Holmes's little friend. Or would you rather be known as Princess Fatima?'

I assumed the best air of dignity possible in the circumstances. 'I have been standing in for Princess Yasmin since she is indisposed. As a favour to both her and her husband. I am sure she will be well again tomorrow.'

He uttered a low chuckle, which ended in a sharp cough. 'You might wonder how I know you. It so happens I have had a conversation with young Orlando Fishwick, who encountered you both recently. Observant boy, he described you both. I have seen Princess Yasmin enough times to know when she is being impersonated. I am, as you might have guessed, Alexander Ashbury, and should you ever decide on a stage career, you should let me know. I can think of a number of acts and locations for which your particular talents would be well suited.'

'Oh, this performance was for one night only, I assure you.'

'I am sorry to hear it. The Indian basket trick is quite a favourite of mine. I have never been able to devise how it is done. And yet here it is, before my eyes, the very thing. Do you really fit inside such a narrow space?'

'Yes, and — well, I cannot say what its secrets are, but it is the easiest thing to get out of. I can do it in moment, and no-one is the wiser.'

He grinned. 'Satisfy my curiosity, Mr Stamford. Show me how it is done.'

Naturally I could not suggest that Mr Ashbury lie in the basket himself, as it was far too small for him, so, wanting to get into his good opinion, I stepped inside and lay down in the receptacle.

'Good, good, very good,' he wheezed. Then he moved much faster than I might have given him credit for, and slammed the lid down, fastening it by the little catch at the front. 'Now show me how you get out.'

And try as I might, I could not.

It is probably not the secret nowadays that it once was, so I can reveal that the Indian basket is a specially constructed device. It has a hinged section along the length of one side, the side the audience cannot see, which enables the person apparently trapped inside to roll out. I had practised this a dozen times, under the instruction of Mr Chandler, but suddenly my escape refused to move. There was only one explanation; Mr Ashbury was standing in the way, the weight of his body holding me prisoner. 'I think, Mr Ashbury, that you might need to move back a little so I can show you how the trick is done,' I said.

He chuckled again, and there was the unmistakable sound of a sword being drawn. 'Do you know, whenever I have seen this done, I had always imagined that the magician's sword was not a real one — that it was a trick blade and did not pierce the basket at all. But now I see that Prince Chandra's sword is in fact quite genuine, very sharp, very slender. By selecting the right location, he can thrust the sword through the woven material of the basket without damaging it. Of course, it would be a serious matter should he do so while someone was actually inside.'

'Yes, it would,' I said, with some feeling. 'Could you let me out now, please?'

'Not yet. Not before we have had a little word.' To my horror, I saw a thin shining blade descend through one of the spaces in the basketwork, moving towards my chest. It was impossible for me to turn aside to avoid it, and I shrank back as far as I could. 'I want you to tell your friend Mr Holmes that he is to keep his prying nose out of my business,' said Ashbury. 'I know he has been hoping to find out about Mr Tapper, and he would like nothing better than to put the blame for Tapper's death on me. But I had nothing to do with it. That night I was meeting with several other gentlemen on a matter of business in another part of London. I didn't kill Tapper and neither did I pay another man to do it. Tapper was a worm, a worthless piece of rubbish. Why should I trouble myself about him?'

It was some slight comfort that if Ashbury wanted me as a messenger, then he would be obliged to leave me alive. 'I'll tell Holmes what you have said, I promise!'

'You do that, or we might be obliged to have another conversation.'

The blade slowly withdrew, but then it stabbed down in a precise manner, not towards my body, but through the lid and the side and into the floorboards, jamming the basket closed. I held my breath, and to my immense relief, heard the sound of the door closing.

And now I had to make my escape. I did think of crying out for help but dreaded the embarrassment of being found in this predicament and in such garments. I hoped, therefore, to be able to escape without assistance. I certainly didn't want to damage any of the Chandlers' costumes and properties, which I would then be obliged to replace out of my own pocket.

I was struggling to open the basket, sweating profusely through the greasepaint, when I heard a knock at the door. A soft voice called out 'Evie?'

I fell silent. My visitor was not Holmes, and neither was it Ashbury returning. Whoever was outside could surely not be any worse than my assailant, unless of course I was about to meet Mr Tapper's killer. I decided not to answer. Then I heard the door open.

'Evie? Are you in there? Let me help you out!'

The visitor had taken hold of the sword, and with something of an effort it was pulled free. The lid of the basket was thrown back, and I looked into the fine blue eyes of Amelie Gaston. The eyes were even lovelier when they opened wide with astonishment. She was wearing a green silk wrap over one of her stage costumes, the one known as the black mamba.

'Oh, Mr Stamford!' she exclaimed. 'You have got yourself in a very strange situation. Where is Evie? Why are you wearing her clothes?'

I crawled from the basket, and she helped me to my feet.

'Mrs Chandler was unwell and is resting at home. Just something she ate; I am sure she will be recovered by tomorrow. Mr Chandler asked me to take her place on stage tonight. But someone came in and played a trick on me.'

My rescuer looked sympathetic. 'Oh, poor Mr Stamford, what a cruel thing to do. But it is the way with some people. Always playing the little tricks. Are you hurt?'

'No, just a little shaken.'

'Here, let me wipe your face. Sit down, and I will take the greasepaint off for you.'

She drew me to the chair so I could sit before the mirror and the little shelf of cosmetics. I could not bear to look at myself, and turned so I could face her. She used some cream from a jar and a sponge to wipe the paint from my face and neck, then poured some water from a little jug into a basin into which she dipped a cloth, and gently washed me clean, which was very refreshing. 'There,' she said with a satisfied smile. 'And now I think I should leave you to dress yourself. When you have done, I will come back and look after Evie's costume.'

I thanked her and was just rising from the seat when Holmes arrived, and Miss Gaston left us. He stared at me with ill-disguised displeasure.

'I was wondering what had delayed you,' he said sternly.

'I was trapped in the basket by Mr Ashbury,' I said.

'I saw he was here. What did he want?'

'He had a message for you. He said he was not responsible for the death of Mr Tapper and was in company with others that night. And he had not ordered anyone else to deal with Tapper. I don't know if he is telling the truth.'

'He is not the most reliable of men,' said Holmes.

'He knows what you look like,' I said. 'Young Orlando described us.'

'That is not a difficulty,' said Holmes, dismissively. 'When I go to see him, I shall adopt a disguise.'

I was still a little shaky on my legs and sat down on a trunk to recover. Quite suddenly, all the anxieties of the past few weeks, which I had not dared to express, came pouring out. 'Holmes,' I said, 'if you don't mind, I must refrain from assisting you for the time being. I have my final examinations very soon, and while I have been careful in my preparations, I need to think of nothing else until they are done. Please — I ask you not to call on my help until I am ready to give it.'

He paused and for a moment I thought he might be disappointed in me, but then his expression softened. 'Of course, I understand,' he said at last. 'I will wait outside until you are dressed and hire a hansom to take you home. In the next weeks I shall devote myself to the study of conjuring and fashioning a means of exposing the crimes of the nefarious Mr Ashbury.'

CHAPTER SEVENTEEN

It would be pleasant to report that this was an important turning point in my friendship with Sherlock Holmes; however, such was not the case. His habit of thoughtlessly commandeering the time of others without warning persists to this day. Fortunately, on this particular occasion, he was sufficiently occupied with his own activities not to require my assistance, or at least he refrained from demanding it. To my enormous relief, I was able to immerse myself in my studies and completed my examinations without interruption. Readers of this memoir will be heartened to know that I passed creditably at the first attempt.

My intention was to occupy myself during the summer months by taking additional courses, the better to prepare myself for the post of junior surgeon, but I was able to find the time to meet with Holmes again, and in a far calmer frame of mind. During all our subsequent conversations, my adventure in the basket was never referred to.

'I have spoken again with Mr Goodgold regarding the tragedy in Bristol,' said Holmes, when we found a quiet retreat for luncheon. 'He did not preserve any material relating to the incident, which I can well understand, but he did recall the date. I quickly located a report in *The Times*, which matched his account. The inquest on the unfortunate Mr Winstone made it clear that the other two volunteers could not be held to blame, as they were merely acting under Tourmalin's direction with materials he provided. While unable to account for what had happened, Mr Goodgold accepted responsibility for Mr

Winstone's death, which went some way to reducing the severity of the charge and the sentence.'

'I am glad we know he was telling us the truth,' I said.

'As far as I have been able to determine, he was, although I do not trust the cat. I think that Mr Goodgold is by nature a truthful and honourable man, and when he is forced to avoid being wholly open, he delegates that task to Archie. But I remain troubled by that affair. Was it a simple error? Or something else?' The implication hung in the air, unanswered.

'I regret that I am no nearer to discovering who tied the ropes around Mr Tapper,' he added. 'There are two main possibilities: a person employed by Mr Ashbury to threaten him into revealing Mr Maskelyne's secrets, or the victim of one of his blackmail schemes. All the persons working at the Egyptian Hall had something to hide. Mr Goodgold admits he paid Tapper for his silence, but denies harming him. The Gastons have freely told me of their past, but do not think a revelation at this time would affect their prospects. Mr Jennings has told me of his nephew's history, but that has never been kept secret from his employers. And only a fool would consider attempting to extort money from Maskelyne and Cooke. I don't believe Mr Chandler is exempt from having secrets, it is just that he has yet to reveal them.'

'Perhaps the answer lies in his past in India,' I said. 'I know he still takes an interest in the administration of that country. He was reading a newspaper about the work of Indian Council.'

'When did you see him do that?' asked Holmes.

'I saw the paper in his dressing room on the day when — the day when Mrs Chandler was taken ill.'

'Ah,' said Holmes. 'The Indian Council, a powerful body, advisors to the government. They meet in Whitehall. I think I shall make a few enquiries.'

I was well aware that Holmes's brother Mycroft worked at the government offices in Whitehall and was a valuable source of information, which he provided in strict confidence.

Holmes had been far from idle in his pursuit of the art of conjuring, as he proceeded to demonstrate. In just a short while he had become proficient in a number of card tricks, sufficiently so that he was confident that he was nearly ready to apply to Mr Ashbury for an audition. I later found that the additional dexterity he gained from this work had served to improve his performance on the violin, and he was able thereafter to coax a tuneful melody from the instrument.

We were subsequently granted some further meetings with Inspector Knight, who supplied us with details of the enquiries about Mr Tapper by the Liverpool police. It had emerged that while Tapper had never married, he had, when in Liverpool, lived with a widow called Mrs Harding, but they had parted company after a disagreement. Efforts were being made to discover her whereabouts. Mr Ashbury's claim to have an alibi for the night of Tapper's death had been checked and confirmed — at least, it could not be shaken. Holmes, however, could not altogether dismiss the idea that Ashbury was involved in some way, and this did not deflect his intention to arrange a face-to-face meeting.

We were able to secure a second interview with Mr Chandler, who appeared curiously unsurprised to be asked to meet with us once more. We gathered in the little gallery. I have to admit to being relieved we were not invited to the dressing room, which held such horrible memories for me.

'I sensed when we last spoke that there was something you were not telling me,' said Holmes, evenly. 'The relations between Britain and India have been undeniably hard for all those who love both countries. On that occasion you mentioned your late father, who had served as a minor official for ten years in India. Yet my enquiries have revealed that there is no man who meets that description. Not precisely. There is a man who spent ten years in India as a senior official and who lived there with his family. He is now a powerful presence in advising the government. He has a son who is your age. I learned that he had great hopes for that son to follow him into the service, but it appears he did not.'

Chandler allowed himself a sad smile. 'Before I say anything further concerning my history, I wish to establish something,' he said. 'I have been told, Mr Holmes, that you have conducted enquiries for some of our major institutions and enjoy their complete confidence that you will not reveal any information which might be sensitive or controversial.'

'That is true,' said Holmes. 'Whatever you reveal to me will be in confidence, and you may also trust Mr Stamford absolutely. What I wish to know is this: is there something that Mr Tapper learned about you — something he used to demand money for his silence? I confess it does seem unlikely that a man in his position would be privy to such information. Please enlighten me, if only so I might set aside all suspicion on the issue and move on with my investigation into more fruitful areas.'

Chandler nodded. 'Tapper knew nothing of a sensitive nature,' he said. 'He made no demands upon me, and I had no reason to harm him. I can advise you that my family name is not Chandler. But from your comments I feel sure you have already discovered that. I have not used my true name since I went on the stage. My father, as you now know, is not deceased, and is of high rank. I concealed the truth to protect him. I was twenty when we returned from India. It was here that I first met Evie. She was just sixteen, and part of a touring troupe of entertainers, appearing in London. Dancing and acrobatics. I fell in love. Who could not love her?' he added wistfully. 'I introduced myself and found her to be as good and charming as she is beautiful. India has many jewels, and she is one. We met in secret and when I told my father I wished to marry her he forbade it. Had she been the daughter of a maharaja I suspect that he might have thought differently, but her humble birth and occupation, although no obstacle to me, did not please my father, who was already seeking a match he thought more suitable. I defied him, of course. As soon as I reached my majority, Evie and I were married.'

'You are estranged from your father?' asked Holmes.

'We have not spoken in some time. He continues to hope that I will see the error of my ways and cast Evie aside. I hope that he will come to understand that it is not a crime to marry for love.'

'Are you his principal heir?'

'No. I have an older brother who was at college when we went to India. He is now a barrister. I would inherit only a younger son's portion, if anything. I suppose Tapper might, if he had known my true parentage, have threatened to expose my situation to the public, embarrassing my family and destroying all hope of a reconciliation. But I promise you, he never learned of it.'

Holmes asked no further questions, and I believe he was content to accept Mr Chandler's explanation. I asked if he had made an appointment to see Mr Ashbury, but he said he needed to arm himself with some additional information before he did so. 'Recall that when Goodgold as Tourmalin started to perform the bullet catch, he did so because of the campaign by Ashbury to promote his own man, Dr Peralta by underhand means. It makes me wonder if Ashbury knew something about what happened, and whether Tapper learned of it. If I can lay Mr Ashbury by the heels, I might arrive at the truth in the Tapper case as well.'

CHAPTER EIGHTEEN

Following the interview with Mr Chandler, Holmes was absent from London for a few days. Once I knew he had returned, I invited him to take supper in my rooms, since I was hoping for an account of his investigations. I had been able to obtain a nice, if rather small, cold roast fowl, and some tomatoes.

'After we last spoke, I consulted the Bristol newspapers held in the British Museum for further enlightenment on the Winstone case,' said Holmes, opening a bottle of beer as I jointed the fowl and buttered some thick slices of bread. 'It so happened that a correspondent attached to a daily newspaper was present in the audience on the night of the tragedy, and he later attended the inquest on Mr Winstone, and the trial of Mr Goodgold. His report was most informative, and several points attracted my attention.

'The volunteer who loaded the pistol before Mr Goodgold fired at the target was a Mr Barrett, a grocer by trade. He attended the inquest and gave evidence there. The second volunteer, however, the man who loaded the pistol before it was fired by Mr Winstone with fatal consequences, was never discovered to give evidence, and his name is unknown. It was thought that he was so shocked by the occurrence that he left the theatre, and such was the consternation that his absence initially went unnoticed, by which time it was too late to question him.'

'He must have thought he had had a lucky escape,' I said. 'If he had agreed to fire the gun, he might have died or been horribly injured. Or did he perhaps fear that he might be blamed?'

'The coroner did not believe that either volunteer should bear any responsibility,' said Holmes. 'I am not so sure. There was an important witness at both the inquest and the trial, a Miss Huggins. I think she was the sister Goodgold told us of. She said she was Tourmalin's housekeeper and assisted him in the preparation and maintenance of the properties used in his performance. This included the trick bullets, which created a smoke effect. She stated with absolute certainty that all the ammunition used had been most carefully prepared, and it was impossible for anything to have exploded or caused any harm. An expert was called who, while he was unable to deduce anything from the fragments, or the remaining unfired ammunition, suggested that Tourmalin had mistakenly loaded the pistol with too large an amount of gunpowder. I feel sure that his evidence was given more weight than that of Miss Huggins.'

There was a pause while we made short work of the fowl, tomatoes and buttered bread. Another bottle of beer was opened, and I brought to the table a fine apple turnover, provided by my mother, who was always concerned about the plight of starving students.

'I therefore decided to go to Bristol to see what I could discover there,' said Holmes. 'Fortunately, I was able to locate the newspaper correspondent who had written the original account of the tragedy, a Mr Brooks. He had over the years maintained a close interest in the affair, and still had the notes he had made on the day. He accepted the coroner's decision that the two volunteers were not to blame. But I learned one important thing. Mr Goodgold had asked the volunteers for their names when they came up onto the stage, and Brooks had made a note of them. The first man was the grocer called Barrett, as we know. The second man gave his name as Potter.

After the explosion the correspondent saw Potter rushing from the theatre, with an expression of horror on his face.'

'Potter?' I exclaimed. 'Was that not the real name of the rival magician, Peralta? Goodgold told us that he had never met Peralta, so if it was he, Goodgold would not have recognised him when he volunteered.'

'Indeed. I thought to ask Mr Brooks if he had ever met Mr Ashbury, and he said he had, and knew of his dubious reputation. Ashbury had been to the newspaper office two weeks before to arrange for a series of advertisements for Peralta, who would shortly be appearing in Bristol. The advertisements confirm that Peralta was performing in Bristol, but on the night of the tragedy he was between engagements.'

'Then he might have been in the audience,' I said. 'Was Ashbury there? I doubt he would have volunteered. And Goodgold had already met him, so he would never have permitted him on stage.'

The apple turnover was consumed, and while as good as any my mother had ever made, I was so engaged with Holmes's news that I scarcely did it justice.

'I was not able to locate Miss Huggins,' Holmes continued, 'but Brooks told me he had spoken to her after the inquest, and she had invited him to their house and showed him how the gun and the bullets were prepared. Every trick bullet used by Tourmalin bore a special mark, the letter H. She even offered to be a target for him, to show that there was no danger in the proceeding. He declined either to fire the gun or to be a target himself. Miss Huggins then fired it at a log of wood, which she did in perfect safety. She was very competent and assured, and he rather thought she had the intention of going on stage herself.'

'I wonder if she did?' I asked. 'A lady performing the bullet catch would be a novelty.'

'There is one such,' said Holmes. 'She goes under the name of Madame Houdina, most probably taking that name in imitation of the late renowned Monsieur Robert-Houdin, and her performance is very similar to that of Tourmalin. She is something of a sensation in France.'

'Does Goodgold know of Madame Houdina and her act?'

'I think they must both consider that any connection between Madame Houdina and Tourmalin should not be made public. I did, however, find and speak to Mr Barrett the grocer,' added Holmes. 'Mr Barrett turned out to be rather a superior kind of grocer since he has about a dozen shops, a fruit bottling factory, a substantial family and a manor house in the leafier environs of Bristol. He is an enthusiast of stage magicians and likes to see all of those who come to Bristol on tour. This included Dr Peralta. He told me he thought the man named Potter greatly resembled Peralta and indeed he wondered if it was in fact he who had volunteered to go on stage in order to spy on his rival's methods, although he did not like to say anything at the time in case he was mistaken. He said nothing on the subject at the inquest as it had been determined that neither volunteer was at fault.'

'Did anyone else have the same suspicions?' I asked. 'Did no-one speak to Peralta afterwards?'

'It appears not, and after the tragedy the newspapers reported that Peralta's subsequent appearances in the city had been cancelled. It was assumed that this was done out of respect to the deceased. I think it more likely that Peralta decided to flee. This incident may have been the start of his decline. His stage name was not associated with the tragedy, so he continued to use it, but it seems likely that he broke away from Mr Ashbury soon afterwards. I am sure that while in Bristol, he was acting on behalf of Mr Ashbury, observing how his rival carried out the bullet catch, perhaps with the intention of replicating it, and then claiming he was superior to Tourmalin. Did he in some way feel responsible? He certainly never performed the trick himself. A wise decision.'

'Perhaps,' I said, 'Peralta, if he was spying for Ashbury, saw something Mr Barrett would not have noticed. Perhaps — oh my word — perhaps he saw something that would have exonerated Goodgold.'

'If he did, then he might have told Ashbury. But Ashbury would never have allowed him to give evidence.'

'No, because Ashbury wanted to undermine Goodgold's career. I think Peralta did the right thing in parting from him. Do you think you can get the truth from Ashbury?'

'I can certainly try. Incidentally, I did discover something from Mr Barrett of the subsequent history of Mrs Winstone. It appears that she paid a visit to him after the inquest to see if he had any further observations. They have remained friends. He spoke of her very admiringly. Following the loss of her husband she devoted herself to the upbringing of her children. They are a credit to her care, but she absolutely refuses to allow them to go to the theatre to see conjuring acts.'

We decided to complete our meal with a small sherry. 'Do you still intend to confront Mr Ashbury? He is a dangerous man.'

'He is, and I can now go fully prepared. I will write to him tomorrow to make the appointment.'

'If you are a conjuror, you must have a stage name.'

'I have been thinking about that. The name Houdina has been taken; but there is always —'

He was interrupted by a knock on the door. 'Another policeman to see you,' my landlady said, gruffly. 'I hope you've not been up to anything?'

I assumed an air of dignity. 'We are professional consultants to the police.' She didn't look convinced and withdrew to admit Inspector Knight. The weather had been cloudy and wet all day, and when he arrived, he was shaking raindrops from his overcoat.

'Ah, gentlemen,' he said, 'I had hoped to find the two of you. Would you be willing to accompany me to the scene of a serious crime?'

We rose to our feet at once.

'It is a case of murder,' he continued, 'and an unusual one at that. And it so happens that the deceased had both your cards in his pocket.'

'His name?' asked Holmes,

'Alexander Ashbury, the theatrical promoter. He has been shot.'

We piled into a waiting carriage and Inspector Knight described the situation as we travelled.

'Mr Ashbury has a little troupe of performers under his control,' he said. 'He hired a set of cheap lodgings for the London season, and they all have rooms there.'

'I know about Oliver Fishwick and his two children,' said Holmes. 'We have spoken to the son and gave him our cards, which must be how Mr Ashbury has them. The boy also mentioned a Monsieur Bonfleur and his wife.'

'Yes, and there is a general maid who lives in as well. Her name is Martha. None of the performers were in the house at the time of the murder, they were all at their places of work. But Martha tells me that Ashbury was expecting a special visitor this evening. Unfortunately, he did not provide a name, only that a gentleman was calling on important business, which required a private meeting. Ashbury told Martha that he would let the visitor in himself, and did not wish to be disturbed; in fact, he said she could go out for the evening if she so wished. Martha duly took the opportunity to invite a young man to accompany her, and he arrived at the house a little while after seven o'clock. A Mr Robinson, who is a plumber by trade. She let him in by the kitchen door, and they were just deciding on where they might go — some nearby hostelry where there was a musical entertainment — when they heard the visitor arrive. Presumably Mr Ashbury went to the door to admit the gentleman as planned. Mr Ashbury's apartments are on the first floor of the house.'

'The maid and her friend did not see the visitor?'

'No, and they could not make out any conversation. As it so happened, they had not yet gone out due to a sudden shower of rain, and while they waited for the weather to clear, they heard noises like two gunshots from the floor above. Alarmed, Martha sent Mr Robinson to run upstairs to Mr Ashbury's rooms and knock on the door, demanding to know if all was well.'

'They did not see another individual in the house, or leaving it?'

'No.'

'Was the door locked?'

'It was. At any rate Mr Robinson was unable to open it. There was no answer from within; however, he did hear sounds of someone inside moving about. As you can imagine, by now Martha was very frightened, and she begged her young man not to break the door down as she thought there might be a desperate man with a gun inside the room. She ran to get a policeman, and Mr Robinson stood guard outside the door ready to apprehend anyone who tried to escape. He is a burly fellow and thought he could knock down the villain before he could shoot him. A few minutes later Martha returned with a constable, who knocked on Mr Ashbury's door. At this time all was silent within, and it was agreed that after giving a warning, the constable and Mr Robinson would force the door open. When the constable entered the room, Mr Ashbury was lying on the floor. He had been shot twice in the chest and was quite dead. The window of the apartment was open. There is a tree outside, close enough for a reasonably agile person to make an escape.'

'What action did the constable take?'

'He sent the maid and her friend to wait in the kitchen and told them to keep all doors locked until he had made his report to the station and fetched assistance. I think they were too frightened to do other than what they were told.'

'I assume the other residents have not yet returned?'

'No, we wouldn't expect them for another hour or so. I questioned the witnesses and searched the body, and that was when I found your cards and thought I would like to see what you make of it.'

I could see that Holmes was rather flattered by this, but he said nothing.

We drew up outside the lodging house, where a uniformed constable in a rain cape stood guarding the front door. It was already dark, and the street was poorly illuminated by flickering gas lamps. There were few people about, and those who were carried umbrellas and were in a hurry to reach their destinations. I suspected that there was little chance of there being any useful witnesses to a murderer making his escape.

We entered a gloomy hallway which smelt of old carpeting and dust. There was no cupboard for coats, just a coat stand, with a receptacle for umbrellas, both empty.

'Are the maid and her friend still here?' asked Holmes as we went upstairs.

'They are, yes,' said Knight.

'I will want to speak to them both when I have seen the room.'

As we knew, Inspector Knight had already interviewed Martha and Robinson, but after a brief hesitation he decided to make no objection.

'Where do the other occupants reside?'

'Mr Fishwick and his son and daughter have the ground floor apartment. Martha has a room next to the kitchen, and Monsieur Bonfleur and his wife the upper room.

As we entered Ashbury's room, I tried to think of what Holmes would be looking for, and endeavoured to see it as he did. The body of the man who had tormented me lay on the floor where he appeared to have fallen, and a doctor stood nearby making some notes. A dead body always draws the eye. In death a person may dominate a room when their surroundings may be equally important.

I looked around. The single gas lamp in the room gave out a dull fitful light. There was the glow of a dwindling coal fire in the grate, and a small coal scuttle, barely half full. The furniture consisted of a made up single bed in one corner, a wooden chair, a small round table on which rested two wine glasses, unused, and a decanter of sherry, as well as some notepaper, pen and ink and an unlit candle in a saucer. There was no wardrobe, only a clothing rail on which hung some bedraggled-looking stage costumes, a colourful dressing gown with a frayed hem, and some shirts which to my eye needed laundering and a hot iron. A small basket contained some tumbled linens. A heavy overcoat of considerable vintage hung on a hook inside the door, together with the Tyrolean hat. There was a single window; the curtains had been drawn apart, and the window was open wide enough for a person to make an exit. Rain spattered through the opening and onto the floorboards.

The most notable thing in the room apart from the late Mr Ashbury lying supine on the rug in front of the fireplace, was his copy of the automaton Psycho, once known as Osric. While it might have been convincing when seen at a distance, viewed close up it was very obviously a poor quality imitation. The body was fashioned from some coarse material, the clothing was made of cheap fabrics, and there was a painted plaster head wrapped in what was meant to be a turban but looked more like a bandage. The damage from its stage conflict was very apparent, as the body leaned drunkenly to one side, and there were rents in the costume from the angry crowd's attempts to tear it open. The box it sat upon was rather wider and broader than the one that supported Psycho, and I felt sure that there was ample room to accommodate young Orlando Fishwick if he put his head and one arm inside the figure. The box was badly dented, the sides were caved in, and the lid broken.

Inspector Knight introduced us to Dr Conway, who was preparing to have the body removed to the police mortuary. 'The deceased was shot twice in the chest,' he said. 'Either shot would have been fatal. One must have pierced the heart and was fired from several feet away. The second one appears to have been fired after he fell, and with the muzzle of the gun pressed against the skin. As you see, the collar of the shirt is open, and the top few buttons undone. This bullet would have pierced the lung. But I will know more when I have recovered the bullets, neither of which passed through the body.'

Holmes stared down at the corpse. 'It appears from the position of the shirt that the first shot was also fired while it was open,' he said.

'Judging by where it passed through the material, I must agree,' said Dr Conway. 'It is an unusual adjustment of clothing in which to greet an invited guest, but perhaps he was in the process of changing his shirt and the guest arrived early.'

Holmes lit his pocket lantern, and examined the markings on the floorboards, damp smears of footprints caused by the rain, and sighed in disappointment at what he knew must be the obliteration of vital clues. He looked out of the window, studying all possible means of egress. There was no drainpipe, or ivy on the walls; however, just outside, within a few feet of the window ledge, the branches of a tree with the beginning of spring growth, waved in the wind.

'There is a mark of a boot on the lower window frame,' said Knight.

'So there is,' said Holmes. 'A partial print made by a damp shoe in the dust, now much occluded by rain. A narrow foot — not Mr Ashbury's.' He studied the window frame. 'Whoever stood there, on just one foot it seems, must have worn gloves when he steadied himself. But I will learn more when I return in daylight.' He completed his examination of the room, which involved a detailed study of the overcoat and hat, all the clothing on the rail, and the surface of the rail itself. He peered underneath the bed, where there was an assortment of boxes and trunks, and more dust than one might have thought acceptable, emerging from this study with his handkerchief over his nose.

'I would like to see what is in those boxes,' he said.

'And you shall, sir, once the police have extracted them and examined the contents,' said Knight, in a tone that admitted no argument.

Holmes nodded without protest, and took a little time to examine Osric, noting as he did so the differences between the copy and the original. Opening the crumpled lid of the box he saw a pile of folded bedsheets, which he scrutinised, finding nothing concealed. He closed the lid and turned to Inspector Knight.

I would like to speak to the maid and her friend now,' he said. 'Kindly have them brought here.' I saw Dr Conway raise an eyebrow at my friend's casual command of the policeman, and he was even more surprised when Knight obligingly went to fetch the witnesses.

Martha was a sturdy woman of about thirty, dressed appropriately for an evening excursion, her swain a solid and respectable-looking fellow of about the same age. Both stared at Holmes, who must have seemed very young to be in the position of consultant.

Holmes began by questioning the maid. 'What time did you light the fires this morning?'

'I go up and do Mr Ashbury's fire at eight o'clock when he is in the kitchen having his breakfast. And I bring up the coals so he can keep it going.'

'When did you last see him?'

'That would have been about five in the afternoon, after he had his tea. He said he was expecting a gentleman to come and see him at about half past seven. It told me it was an important meeting, and he didn't want to be disturbed.'

'Do you know if he received a letter or a note making the appointment?'

'Yes, there was a note.'

'Did you see the note?'

'He had it in his hand when he spoke to me. I didn't see what was written on it. I don't think he wanted me to see it.'

'What did he do with the note?'

'I can't be sure, but I think he put it in his pocket.'

Holmes glanced at Inspector Knight who shook his head, from which I gathered that the note had not been found on the body.

'I would like you to take a look around the room and tell me if anything is missing that is usually here or has been moved since you last saw it.'

Martha nodded, and looked about her, but at last she said, 'I don't think anything has been taken.'

'What about the clothing rail? Has anything been removed from it?'

'No, I don't think so. The fancy costumes are always there, and the dressing gown and the shirts. He doesn't have many clothes. Just the one overcoat that's hanging on the door, and the suit he is wearing.'

'He usually keeps the coat on the hook on the door?'

'Yes.'

'Take a look under the bed. Has anything been taken or moved about?'

Martha peered under the bed but when she rose, she shook her head. 'Mr Ashbury said I wasn't to move his boxes. He said his best things were in them. I don't know what they are.'

'Which explains the dust,' murmured Holmes. 'What about Osric, here?'

'Oh, that awful thing! Mr Ashbury said it was his top money-maker and he was going to spruce it up and do some repairs so he could work it again.'

'Thank you, Martha,' said Holmes. He turned to the man. 'Mr Robinson, what time did you arrive here?'

'It was a bit after seven.'

'And you came to the kitchen door?'

'I did.'

'Did you both hear the visitor arrive?'

Robinson nodded, and Martha said, 'Yes, there's a bell rings in the kitchen, and a knocker as well. But I didn't go to let him in as Mr Ashbury said not to.'

'What time was that?'

'It would have been about half past seven.'

'Did either of you see the visitor?'

'No.'

'Can you say how long it was between the visitor arriving to hearing the shots?'

Robinson gave this some thought. 'It's hard to say. It wasn't long. Just a few minutes.'

Martha nodded agreement. 'We thought we ought to wait inside a bit before we went out, as the rain had started coming down harder. We hoped it might let up.'

'The rain had been quite light up to then?' asked Holmes.

'Yes,' said Robinson. 'When I walked up to the house it was very light.'

'Can you remember how much time elapsed between the first and second shot?'

Both looked thoughtful. 'We didn't think it was a shot at first,' said Robinson. 'Martha said, "What's that? Is it lightning?" And I said it sounded like a gun going off, but Martha said, "No, Mr Ashbury won't allow guns." I said it might be one of those trick guns, like the ones magicians use, and the visitor was showing it to him. Then we heard it again, and I said, "I think it's a gun".'

'That's when you went upstairs,' said Martha.

'Now this is very important,' said Holmes. 'In the time between hearing the second shot and going upstairs, did either of you hear the visitor leave? Might he have run down the stairs and out of the front door?'

Martha and her friend considered this, and both shook their heads. 'We didn't hear anything,' said Martha.

'And was the front door open or closed?'

'Closed. I would have noticed if it was stood open in that weather.'

'What did you do then?'

'I went up the stairs,' said Robinson, 'and when I got to the top I called out to Mr Ashbury. I said, "Is everything all right, Mr Ashbury?" When there was no answer I went up to his room and knocked at the door. There was still no answer, so I took the handle and rattled it, but the door wouldn't open. Then I thought I heard someone inside the room.'

'What kind of noise did you hear?'

'Just someone moving about. I couldn't tell what they were doing.'

'What happened then?'

'I called down to Martha. She was standing at the bottom of the stairs. She said I shouldn't go in the room in case something bad had happened. So I told her to run for a policeman and I would stand at the door until she came back.'

'I was only gone about ten minutes,' said Martha.

Mr Robinson nodded agreement to this. 'And I never left the door.'

'Did you hear the window being opened?'

'I heard a lot of thunder.'

'Anything else?'

'No.'

'One more question, Martha,' said Holmes, turning to the maid. 'Does Mr Ashbury own an umbrella?'

'Yes.'

'And where does he keep it? I don't see one in this room.'

'It's usually in the hall stand.'

'It isn't there now,' said Holmes.

'Oh? Is it not? It was there before.'

'I could not help noticing that although you went out to find a policeman in the heavy rain, your bonnet and upper garments are not wet,' said Holmes. 'And while the umbrella stand is empty there are some drops of moisture in there. Did you borrow the umbrella to protect your gown and bonnet from the rain when you went out?'

'Well, yes, I did. But when I came back, I made sure to shake it out well. I'm sure I put it back in the hall stand.'

Inspector Knight grunted. 'I'll see what the constable says. He might have borrowed it, in which case I shall make sure it is returned.'

'Please do,' said Holmes. 'It is a small point, but one I would like cleared up.'

'We think the murderer must have escaped through the window,' Knight continued. 'He might have been under the impression that he and Mr Ashbury were alone in the house for their meeting. Perhaps when he arrived, Ashbury said something to the effect of "I have sent the maid out so we won't be disturbed". After shooting Mr Ashbury he must have searched the body to recover the note, but by the time he had done so, he heard Mr Robinson calling out. He had no alternative but to leave by the window and climb down the tree. I think a young, agile person could have done it. The police have gone round to look at the back with their lanterns, but there is nothing to see at present. There is some paving at the back and a lot of mud.'

'And a great many footprints, I presume,' said Holmes. 'At least when I look tomorrow in the light, I should be able to distinguish regulation police boots from the one which left this print on the window frame. And then I hope to be able to tell you how I believe the murderer made his escape.'

CHAPTER NINETEEN

The next morning was mercifully dry. We returned to the lodging house, where, accompanied by Inspector Knight, we walked about the rear of the building.

'In view of recent events at the Egyptian Hall, and a possible connection to the Tapper case, I have had enquiries made there,' said Knight. 'I have been informed that only one of the performers at the Egyptian Hall, Mr Goodgold, has ever encountered Mr Ashbury in the past and those who know him only by reputation do not think well of him. None of them appears to have a motive to murder him — detest and shun him, yes, but not actually eliminate him. None have had a personal or professional connection to him. All have now been interviewed and I am satisfied that they all have alibis for the time of the murder, having been at the theatre preparing for the evening performance. Checking equipment, doing exercises, costuming, applying greasepaint, and so forth. Also, none of the people I have interviewed have clothes or boots stained with mud, which I think would have been inevitable given the only means of escape in last night's weather. The only person in possession of a gun was the conjuror, Monsieur Gaston. It was unloaded, and there was no sign it had been recently fired. It seems he bought it when he and his sister were very young and began to tour as performers and had no adult protector.'

'Is it possible for the bullets extracted from the deceased to be matched to any type of gun?' I asked.

'The weapon was a small calibre revolver of a very common type that can be purchased anywhere,' said Knight. 'That is all we can deduce.'

'I have been wondering about the second shot made with the muzzle of the gun against the skin,' I said. 'Perhaps it was done when the murderer was searching the body for the note? Even after death a body can exhale a final breath which might be mistaken for a sign of life. If that happened when the murderer was leaning over the body after firing the first shot, he might have been panicked into a second shot, just to make sure.'

'That is a useful observation, and I will consider the possibility,' said Knight.

We trudged carefully about, since the mud had scarcely begun to dry. Looking up towards the window and the branches of the tree, I could see that a person desperate to escape the house might have been able to reach the branches or leap to seize hold of them, and slither down to the ground below. Unfortunately, none of the slender boot prints which might have revealed the flight of the murderer were apparent, having been churned up by larger searching boots, and further overnight rain. Holmes used his glass to examine the trunk of the tree, and to my surprise, essayed a climb to the lower branches, which he also studied. Then he allowed himself to slide down the trunk to the ground and studied the marks his boots had made. Finally, he made a detailed study of the wall of the house for any other possible means of escape.

Returning to the murder room, he studied in full daylight the single boot print on the window frame, measuring its width with a tape measure he had brought. Given the narrowness of the frame there was little enough to see, no heel or toe mark, just the imprint in the dust.

'What do you think, Holmes?' I asked.

'I think,' he said, 'that the murderer did not leave by the window.'

'What?' I exclaimed.

'But there is really no other way,' said Knight.

'I have examined the upper branches of the tree,' said Holmes. 'Not only are they undamaged, but they are also very slender, and could not have held much weight. Also, due to the rain, they would have been very slippery, and hard to grasp. I think the murderer opened the window to judge whether it was possible to leave that way, placing one foot on the frame as he did so, and decided that it was too dangerous. The imprint shows an even pressure of the foot. Had he launched himself forward there would be a change in pressure towards the toe end of the foot.'

'Then how did he escape?' I asked.

'One possibility is that once the door had been broken open, he was able to quickly conceal himself behind it. It is an old trick, but it often works. The constable looked in, saw a body and an open window and made the obvious conclusion. The constable told Martha and Mr Robinson to return to the kitchen and wait while he reported to the station. The broken door could no longer be secured. That was the murderer's opportunity to leave the house without being seen.' Holmes turned to Inspector Knight. 'Did the constable borrow Mr Ashbury's umbrella?'

'He says he did not,' said Knight.

'Has the umbrella been found?'

'Not yet.'

'I think the murderer took it when he left. Locating it could be a vital clue.'

Knight looked thoroughly disgruntled by this. 'I'll ask the maid if there are any marks on it to distinguish it from all the other umbrellas in London,' he said. 'And I'll speak to the constable again. If he missed a murderer hiding behind a door and let him escape, he will have learned a lesson he will never forget.'

'That was a remarkable deduction,' I said to Holmes later when we were back at his rooms, warming ourselves with hot cocoa. 'The inspector was quite certain that the murderer had left by the window.'

'It was simplicity itself,' replied Holmes airily. 'All the signs were there if one cared to observe them. The moisture in the hall stand revealed that a recently used umbrella had been placed there. Martha and Mr Robinson did not leave the house after she returned with the constable, and given that the constable had a rain cape and a helmet, I doubted that he would have commandeered an umbrella for his walk to the station. The only individual who could have left the house, taking the umbrella with him, was the murderer. The conclusion is that when the door was broken open and the body found, he was still in the room.'

'Behind the door?'

'An act of desperation, but effective. He did not hide under the bed, that much was obvious from my examination of that area. The dust was undisturbed. No-one had crawled under there or moved the boxes. I look forward to learning what they contain.'

'I rather think that Mr Ashbury's demise will be little mourned,' I said.

'Yes, and his death was deliberate — every last detail had been planned. It was not a sudden impulse, but an execution. The killer made the appointment for a time when the other occupants of the house would have been absent. Their performance times were advertised in the newspapers. Clearly the murderer knew his victim, and employed a ruse to ensure a private meeting. Perhaps a proposed trade of valuable secrets; a celebrated performer seeking to abandon his current promoter in favour of Mr Ashbury; or a novel act he wished to demonstrate.

'He killed without hesitation, and maintained a cool head, searching the body for the note making the appointment. We would know a great deal more if we had it; in fact, if I was to examine it, I would know the identity of the killer.'

'No doubt from the paper, or the handwriting,' I said.

Holmes nodded. 'But the one thing he could not command was the weather. The sudden heavy downpour meant that Martha and her friend, who were supposed to be absent, were still at the house. When Mr Robinson called out to Mr Ashbury, the murderer must have realised that he was not alone in the house. He would have overheard the conversation between Martha and Mr Robinson and knew that a man would be standing guard outside the door, and escape would be difficult if not impossible. He opened the window, and was faced with torrential rain and slippery tree branches that were unlikely to bear his weight. He was trapped in the room with the corpse of his victim.'

'Had it not been raining, would escape by the window have been possible?'

'That depends on the weight and agility of the killer. But had he done so, I would have seen some damage to the smaller branches and there was none.'

I recalled the acts advertised in the handbills found in Mr Tapper's possession, and a thought occurred to me. 'A performing monkey!' I exclaimed.

Holmes stared at me quizzically.

'Remember the monkey called Blondin,' I said. 'Supposing the murderer had such an animal. They can be trained to do all kinds of things. He writes to Ashbury asking to show it to him. It is a marvel which will make his name. He arrives with the monkey and takes it up with him to Mr Ashbury's room. He opens the window on some pretext or other. Then he leaves the house unseen and waits below, under the tree. The monkey shoots Mr Ashbury, throws the gun down to his master, secures the note and leaps from the window, sliding down the tree.'

Holmes was silent for a while. 'I appreciate that the slender branches of the tree would enable the escape of a monkey,' he said at last. 'But as for the rest — would such a small creature be capable of firing a gun with such accuracy? Or at all? I fear the report might make it drop the weapon.'

'I see what you mean,' I said. 'A larger animal? One of the apes?'

'An orangutan perhaps?'

'Maybe.'

Holmes chuckled. 'And Ashbury had to be shot as he was too large a gentleman to be thrust up the chimney.'

I was on the point of agreeing before I sensed that I was being mocked. I knew that Holmes, in his wide reading, was familiar with the works of Poe, and unlike the public, had a poor opinion of the skills of Poe's detective, Dupin. It ought to be said that despite his casual dismissal of my theory, Holmes was not above seeking such solutions in his subsequent cases. He was willing to consider that the perpetrator was not human, or a human of unusual dimensions. I might even have been the first person to suggest such a thing to him.

'Such a creature would have left some sign of its presence,' Holmes continued. 'The mark of a bare foot, some hairs clinging to the branches. I saw nothing of that kind, either inside or outside the room.' He paused. 'Nevertheless...' He trailed off, and I gathered that he would soon be lighting a contemplative pipe.

CHAPTER TWENTY

Once the post-mortem examination of the deceased had taken place, we attended the inquest, which took place at the coroner's court in Mount Street, near Grosvenor Square. In those early days Holmes liked to attend inquests if it was at all possible. Before becoming a professional detective, they often provided his first glimpse of the persons who had an interest in the case, and he was able to hear the evidence at its freshest. Unfortunately, once he had risen to eminence, he was often called in on cases after the inquest had taken place and had to make do with reports. John Watson's memoirs, while recording Holmes's study of inquests, do not mention attendances. I am sure there must have been some which his 'Boswell' thought too dull to report in any depth, as they simply confirmed his subject's conclusions. The inquest on Mr Ashbury was rather different.

Other than the usual representatives of the press, anxious to wrest all the drama they could from the murder, and members of the public, some of whom frequently attended inquests in preference to the theatre, there were several attendees with a personal interest.

Inspector Knight was good enough to point out those we had not yet encountered. A middle-aged couple were Monsieur and Madame Bonfleur, who had occupied the upper apartment at the lodging house. A substantial man with a ponderous expression and a moustache to match was the landlord. Positioned on the end of the row of public seating was an elderly gentleman with a white beard and hair, sitting very still and erect. Beside him was a much younger professional-looking gentleman. 'Ashbury senior, and his solicitor,' said Knight.

Dr Conway the police surgeon gave a detailed report of the injuries suffered by the deceased. He confirmed that there had been two gunshots. One had been fired from a distance of several feet, undoubtedly from within the room. The bullet had entered the heart, causing immediate collapse and death within moments. The second shot had been fired most probably while the deceased lay on the floor, and an obvious contact wound showed that the muzzle of the gun had been placed against the skin.

There was no evidence of the body having been moved from the position where it had been found.

There was one unusual finding which he could not explain. He had discovered an old injury which could not have played a part in the victim's death, although it did affect his state of health. He had been told that the deceased had often wheezed for breath and was thought to have once suffered a serious affliction of the lungs. He had discovered scarring to one lung, signs that there had once been an injury there, and a possible infection which had destroyed part of the lung tissue.

The coroner leaned forward with interest. 'Do you mean he had been shot before?'

'No, I don't think it was a shooting. At least, there was no track like that of a bullet. I have seen many such and am quite confident about that. It was more like a stabbing with a pointed object. No trace of the object remained, so it would have been withdrawn. I didn't see an external scar. There must have been one once, but it might have been obliterated by one of the gunshots.'

Inspector Knight gave evidence regarding the bullets, which had been extracted from the corpse and subjected to examination. 'The bullets were of a small calibre, and it is probable that both were fired from the same weapon, a revolver of a type easily acquired. Not a military weapon which would be larger, but a civilian model, which could easily have been brought to the scene and taken away concealed in a coat pocket. The room was searched very thoroughly. No weapon of any kind was found. There was no evidence that any other shots had been fired.'

We paid close attention to the evidence of Constable Lewis, the first policeman at the scene. He spoke with sturdy confidence, giving the impression that he was an officer of some experience. Lewis reported being called by the maid to go to the house as there was concern about the safety of her employer. He had hurried there in her company and going up to the first floor found Mr Robinson standing guard outside the door to Mr Ashbury's rooms. They had tried the door, which was locked, and then knocked and demanded entry.

'Did you hear any noise inside the room?' asked the coroner.

'No, although it was hard to hear anything because of the rainstorm. But I don't believe there was any movement inside and I did not hear any voices.'

'I understand that you and Mr Robinson forced the door?'

'Yes, we did.'

'And you saw no living soul in the room?'

'That is so. I saw the body of the deceased lying on the floor, his head towards the fireplace, feet pointing towards the door. The curtains had been drawn apart and the window was open, which I thought very unusual, as it was raining heavily at the time.'

'Did you form the conclusion that Mr Ashbury had been killed by a person who had made his escape through the window?'

'I thought it a strong possibility, based on what I saw.'

'It has been suggested to me that the murderer might have been hiding in the room, standing behind the door.'

There was a muffled snigger from the press.

The constable glanced briefly at Inspector Knight. 'I have been asked about that,' he said with solid dignity. 'I have only made that mistake once, several years ago, and I have a lump on my skull to prove it. I did look behind the door and there was no-one there. There was an automaton — it looked like Psycho, but it wasn't — and it was only so high.' He gestured with his hands. 'I also looked behind the garments on the clothing rail in case there was someone hiding behind them, and underneath the bed, where there was nothing but a great deal of dust and a few boxes, and the usual vessel one finds under a bed.'

'Did you look in the boxes?'

'I did not. None were of a size that could have concealed a person, which was my main concern. There was no-one in the room. When I examined the window, I saw the footprint. I was sure that someone must have climbed out.'

The coroner had no further questions of the witnesses. The verdict of the inquest was that Alexander Ashbury had been murdered by a person or persons unknown, and the proceedings were closed. Ashbury senior and his solicitor hurried away before the pressmen could intercept them.

Inspector Knight went to have a word with the constable, and Holmes approached and was introduced. 'Constable Lewis,' he said, 'your evidence is extremely valuable since you were the first person to examine the scene, and I compliment you on your thoroughness. Might I be permitted to ask some questions?' Lewis glanced at the inspector, who nodded.

'Once the door was broken open, did Mr Robinson enter the room?'

'No, sir, he would have done, but I told him to wait outside.'

'And when you very sensibly looked behind the door, was there a coat hanging there?'

The constable wrinkled his nose in recollection. 'Yes, there was, a very frowsy old coat. I think the moths had been at it. There was no-one inside it or behind it, if that is what you might be thinking.'

Holmes nodded. 'You mentioned looking behind the clothing rail in case the murderer had thought to hide behind it?'

'I did, and there was no-one there.'

'Can you describe what garments you saw on the rail that might have hidden an intruder?'

'An old dressing gown, some things that looked like stage wear, very brightly coloured. And an overcoat.'

'An overcoat?'

'Yes.'

'Do you recall the colour of the coat?'

'It was a plain gentleman's coat. Either black or dark grey.'

Holmes thanked the constable. He appeared calm but I sensed that his mind was busily reviewing this new information and its importance.

'I don't remember seeing a coat on the clothing rail,' said Knight, with a frown.

'That is because there was not one there when we entered the room,' said Holmes, enigmatically. 'I knew that something was missing. It only remained to discover what it was.'

Before I could ask how he had made this deduction, Inspector Knight spoke again.

'I'll have another word with the maid and her fancy man,' he said. 'They both say they never left the kitchen while the constable was away making his report, but I wouldn't put it past either of them to go up to the room and see what they could pilfer while the constable was out.' He shook his head. 'In fact, we only have their word that there was a visitor at all. The whole thing could have been down to them. Mr Robinson looks like a handy type. He might have known how to make the door look like it was locked from the inside.'

'Is that your current line of enquiry?'

'One of several, I am afraid. Mr Ashbury was not good at making friends. I have been looking for a possible financial motive, but all our enquiries so far have shown that Ashbury was no miser hoarding his gold. He seems to have operated on the edge of money troubles. The rent of the lodging house where they have been for the last two months is a month in arrears and Martha hasn't received her wages. The other occupants have been given notice by the landlord to leave at the end of the week.'

'What was in the boxes under the bed?'

'Oh, all sorts of paraphernalia of the conjuring business. Bits of paper and string and wire, and little caskets with trick compartments. It didn't look valuable, but you never know with these things. I was thinking of asking a conjuror to take a look, but I would have to find one who didn't have a motive to kill Ashbury. All I can tell you is that the boxes hadn't been opened or moved for some time. We have completed a search of the entire house, and we did not find either a gun or Mr Ashbury's umbrella.'

'Had he made a will?'

'Not that we have found. Next of kin is his father. Landlord of the Fallow Deer public house out Chingford way. Respectable business. I have spoken to him, and he had no suggestions as to why his son had been killed or who might have done so. I gathered that there hadn't been a great deal of contact between them in the last few years, and he had never been happy with his son's choice of business. He had been hoping his son would tire of the theatre and take over the running of the public house. There is a family plot in Walthamstow and the funeral will take place there with a reception in Chingford. I shall attend, of course.'

'If I might be permitted to attend also?'

'Of course, I'm sure he won't object. I'll let you know the day and time. Oh, and the Liverpool police have spoken to Mrs Harding, Mr Tapper's former lady friend. According to her, Tapper had offered to marry her, but she had refused him because he had no money, and she thought he only wanted to wed her because she had some property. Tapper had told her that he had some business in London which would earn him a good sum but wouldn't say what it was. She wanted to know what money was found in his home and if she could make a claim on it as a common-law wife. The police told her it was not a large amount, and she had no claim. She was in Liverpool at the time of his death, and we have ruled her out as a suspect.'

As we left the court, I asked Holmes what he thought of the evidence, in particular that of Constable Lewis.

'There is much to digest. I am sure you must imagine that I am disappointed that my initial idea, that the murderer had concealed himself behind the door, was incorrect. But in fact, I am not. The evidence of the constable only directs me more keenly to quite another conclusion.'

'You know who killed Ashbury?'

'I believe I know who and how. All I need to establish now is why.'

CHAPTER TWENTY-ONE

It was imperative that Holmes secure an interview with Mr Fishwick without delay, but he was a hard man to locate. The last known place where he had been conducting séances as Prospero no longer featured him, and the proprietor did not know where he was now performing. At the lodging house, where Martha was busy packing her trunk prior to leaving, we learned that Fishwick and the Bonfleurs were out seeking new accommodation and management. When we next went to the house, it was locked up. We discovered where the Bonfleurs were performing and left a message for them requesting an interview. It was three days before we received a reply.

'To be truthful,' said Monsieur Bonfleur, or Harry Flowers, as he was known to his friends, 'we had been very unhappy about Mr Ashbury's style of management for some time.'

We were sitting in a café where that gentleman and his lady wife had agreed to meet us, most probably in hopes of receiving refreshment. Indeed, tea and bread and butter and jam were disappearing at an alarming rate.

'Tell me more,' said Holmes.

'He did not pay anyone on time,' said Mrs Flowers, sharply. 'I have heard rumours that some of his clients were not paid at all and had to sue him. We have seen not a penny from him so far, and now I suppose we never will.'

'You received accommodation as part of your fee?' asked Holmes.

'Such as it is, and a few coals, and breakfast of a sort, but we had to find for ourselves otherwise. Mr Ashbury was known for his meanness — we found that out too late. If he was killed by a creditor there will be too many suspects to count,' said Mrs Flowers.

'He promised a great deal, but delivered little,' said her husband, sadly. 'Once this engagement was done, which it would have been in a few weeks from now, we intended to cease our association with him. We have already met with another gentleman, a Mr Archer, who has a reputation for fairness and honesty. And he has found us somewhere to stay. It is small, but clean. We have already removed from that dreadful house, and Fishwick has as well.'

'It appears that Mr Ashbury was not killed during a robbery,' said Holmes. 'He owned nothing of any value, aside from a number of boxes with materials used in the art of conjuring. Did you ever see them?'

The couple exchanged glances. 'The thing is,' said Flowers, 'we always knew he had some things, but he never allowed us to see them. Then the police released all his possessions, and his father came to take them away. We had a word with him, and asked if we could have the conjuring properties, as they were of no use to him. We offered to pay; we could have scraped together something and paid by the week, but he said we could have them, and he didn't want any money. I think he reckoned that if his son had been in the beer-selling business, he would still be alive.'

'Was there anything of value?'

'Not really,' said Mrs Flowers. 'There were a few costumes that won't fit us. We gave them to Mr Fishwick. Some pieces we can paint up and use. And there were some paper roses.' She smiled. 'They will be very useful.'

'What about Osric?' I asked.

'He is something of a novelty,' said Flowers, 'but I fear his day may be done. The public has learned to be suspicious of imitators of Psycho.'

'Can you tell me what you recall about the night of the murder?' asked Holmes.

'We were working at the time,' said Flowers. 'The doors open at half past seven, and the performances start at eight. We have two sets, one in the first act and one in the second. We are generally there at seven as we have to see to costumes and make-up, also I like to check the properties and the stage machinery to ensure that all is in perfect order. There are any number of persons who can attest to the fact of our presence there on the night Mr Ashbury was killed.'

'Is there anyone you suspect of being involved in the murder?' asked Holmes.

'I don't want to name names,' said Flowers. 'Ashbury had made a lot of enemies over the years.'

'There is a difference between someone a person might want to sue and someone a person wants to murder,' said Holmes.

'Well, I can assure you we know nothing about it,' said Mrs Flowers. 'I am not sorry he has gone, but I wouldn't have troubled myself to hasten it. And we would have been free of him shortly in any case.'

'He told a great many lies,' said Flowers. 'He lied to us and all his advertisements were lies. He liked to make out that Osric was a real automaton. And little Orlando having to crouch inside it and make it move.'

Mrs Flowers shook her head sorrowfully. 'Those poor children,' she sighed. 'I know Fishwick did his best for them, but they had to work hard to make ends meet.'

'Ashbury was intending to get Osric repaired and change its clothes and send it out again under another name,' said

Flowers. 'But Fishwick would have nothing to do with it after what happened — I suppose you heard about that? Ashbury wanted to find someone else who had a child he could put in the box. Dreadful man.'

'And once anyone fell out with him, he would try and cross them so as to promote his own people,' said Mrs Flowers.

'Cross them?' asked Holmes.

'Bad mouth them, say they were no good. He once paid a man to take the screws out of a cabinet, so it fell apart on stage, and made the conjurer look foolish.'

Holmes looked pensive and I suspected he was thinking about Ashbury using Orlando Fishwick to tamper with Psycho. 'Do you know why he was so against the use of guns?' he asked.

Mrs Flowers hesitated. 'I heard once that something bad had happened. Either to him or someone he knew; I can't remember which. I asked him about it, but he wouldn't tell me anything. All I know is he would never agree to any of his acts doing a gun trick.'

'Were you ever acquainted with a Mr Potter who performed as Dr Peralta?'

'No, but I once heard Mr Ashbury say Mr Potter was addicted to drink and had funny ideas. I think they must have had a falling out. Fishwick knows more about him than we do, but he might not want to talk about it.'

'Did they know each other?' asked Holmes, surprised. 'I thought Fishwick didn't work for Ashbury until about two years ago. That was long after Peralta had broken with him.'

'No, Fishwick first worked for Ashbury ten years ago. He used to help out with all the fetching and carrying. That was when he first met Peralta. But he had to give it up when the boy was born, as he was hardly paid anything, and his wife didn't want him going away from home. Two years ago, he came back. I think his wife ran off with another man. That was when he worked up that act with Osric. Peralta had broken off with Ashbury long before, but he and Fishwick still saw each other. They were friends. Fishwick was very cut up when Peralta died. He said Ashbury had driven him to it.'

'What kind of an act did Peralta do?'

'Oh, cards and coins. Changing the colour of water. Pulling flowers out of a hat. Silks ... he liked to use silks. They looked good on stage. That was how he died. Strangled himself with one of his own silks.'

I was astonished to hear that. 'Is it possible to strangle oneself?'

'Well, he was a conjurer — I'm sure he found a way.'

'Did Peralta ever perform the bullet catch?' asked Holmes.

'Oh, no, never. He didn't like guns either. Did you hear about Tourmalin? Tourmalin was a conjuror, who tried to outdo Peralta by performing that gun trick. But then look what happened — Tourmalin made a mistake and killed someone.'

'I had heard of it. Were you told why Peralta broke with Ashbury?'

'No. I expect Fishwick knows.'

'I would like to talk with Mr Fishwick. Where can he be reached nowadays?'

Mr and Mrs Flowers glanced at each other.

'We're not to say,' said Flowers. 'This whole thing has upset him. He said he doesn't want to talk to anyone. I expect he will do, in time. But —' Flowers paused before continuing — 'you might like to go and see Prospero the Mystic with his Cabinet of Wonders in a room above the Oak Leaf public house in Covent Garden. Every night at eight o'clock, one shilling.'

We thanked them, and Holmes provided his card. 'If you should learn any more, please let me know at once,' he said.

'The Cabinet of Wonders,' mused Holmes, as we made our way to Covent Garden.

'Perhaps it will reveal the truth,' I said.

'That would be a rare wonder indeed,' said Holmes.

The Oak Leaf was one of the smaller hostelries in an ancient thoroughfare. Though barely wide enough for a carriage, there was constant traffic passing through, since it linked two busy locations, the marketplace to the north, and Strand to the south. It was a street we knew well, since Holmes and I often attended the gymnasium above the much larger King Henry Tavern. Here, boxing master Professor Logan reigned supreme, and we took classes in sparring.

The Oak Leaf, which was at the northern end, presented a narrow frontage and a single entrance door, beside an alleyway plunged into semi darkness. The name 'Grundy' appeared as licensee above the door. Holmes studied the exterior, which did not look inviting. 'I have been to worse places,' he confessed.

I am not sure if that was meant to be comforting. His enquiries in Bermondsey last winter, during excursions at which I had not been present, had left him badly bruised.

In the shelter of the doorway was a poster advertising 'Prospero the Mystic and his Cabinet of Wonders. 8pm nightly. One shilling. Upstairs.' It was enlivened by a crudely hand-drawn portrait of a man clad in wizardly robes wielding a wand. Ghostly figures, suggested by wavy lines, appeared to be flowing from the wand.

We pushed open the door. It was remarkably quiet for a drinkers' den, and the men who gathered there, who I guessed were in the trade of deliveries or worked on the market, did not appear to be concerned about the marvels that were to be enacted above.

An arrow painted on the wall directed us to a set of creaking wooden stairs to a landing on the floor above, where another Prospero poster was affixed to a door. The stairs continued to ascend to the floor above but were roped off.

As we entered the domain of Prospero, I realised that we had not as yet met Mr Fishwick, and I wondered if he was as impressive a presence as the drawing suggested.

We were met at the door by a young girl, in an old-fashioned gown that was too large for her, and much mended. She was very thin, and the billowing pale gauze that enveloped her made her appear almost transparent, as if there was nothing solid about her form. If she was, as I suspected, eleven-year-old Jessica Fishwick, she was rather small for her age, but her face was older, with an expression of unflinching determination. 'That will be a shilling each, gentlemen,' she said, holding out a cup. 'This way to see the wonders of Prospero and his magic cabinet.'

We made our payments and were permitted to enter. The room was longer than it was wide and was illuminated only by the low flicker of a gas lamp.

There were two rows of chairs, about a dozen in all, facing the far wall, in which was a door. Only four of the chairs were occupied, by two gentlemen and two ladies. Two curtained windows were doing their best to exclude any light from the street. We sat down on the second row.

I stared at the door, which gave no hint of what lay beyond, but I could not help but suspect that it was the entrance to a broom cupboard. I glanced at my pocket watch. It was five minutes to eight.

At eight o'clock, there being no further arrivals, the girl closed the entrance to the room and went to stand by the door. She carried a bell, which she rang, before extinguishing the last glimmers of the gas lamp. As our eyes adjusted to the gloom, we were able to make out only the shape of her slight form. 'Ladies and gentlemen,' she announced, 'behold the Cabinet of Wonders.'

She opened the door. I had expected darkness within, but there was actually a phosphorescent glow, which hovered in the darkness like the moon. This light was emitted by a scattering of archaic symbols culled from a variety of sources, Greek, astrological and mathematical, and little stars, which appeared to float in the air, but must have been affixed to a curtain. 'As you see, the cabinet is quite empty,' said the girl, waving a hand about the interior to demonstrate that there was no-one inside.

She closed the door and knocked on it. 'And now, behold Prospero!' she cried and flung the door open. The figure of a man was now standing inside, and he stepped into the room with a flourish. He was a diminutive, slender individual, wearing shabby evening clothes, a shoulder cape dusted with something that shimmered, and a top hat. He carried a wand.

'Ladies and gentlemen,' he said, bowing to the audience, 'I am indeed the wizard Prospero, and this, my wonderful cabinet, contains marvels that can be seen nowhere else.'

He made elaborate movements in the interior of the cabinet with his wand, then he closed the door and struck it three times whilst uttering some words in a language I did not recognise. Finally, he exclaimed, 'Behold Trinculo!' When the door opened, it revealed a very small jester in cap and bells. The figure leaped into the room and did a capering dance, which was greeted with amusement. Prospero pointed his wand at the cabinet, and when the girl stepped inside, he closed the door. The jester entertained us for a while with his dance, although he told no jokes or riddles, before Prospero tapped on the door and opened it to show us that the cabinet was once again empty. It was now the jester's turn to vanish inside the cabinet, and he was replaced by a queenly figure, radiantly gowned, with a crown on her head, who walked before the audience resplendent in royal dignity. On the next transformation, the cabinet, which appeared to be full of many figures, or possibly the same two figures in different costumes, now displayed a long-tailed monkey, which leaped out and ran about the room, twisting its form into curious shapes, the ladies present obligingly greeting its antics with squeals of laughter.

'And now,' said Prospero, once the monkey had retired to whence it had come, 'I will call up the spirit that haunts this hostelry. Do not be afraid, I beg of you, for he is a pious and benevolent soul. He was once a noble knight who stayed here on his way to a perform a holy quest.' He tapped the cabinet door again. It appeared at first to be empty, then the curtain at the back of the cabinet parted and a glowing face appeared, peeping through its folds, some six feet from the floor. It was not a mask, but an actual face, since it moved its eyes and mouth in strange grimaces.

'Come forth, sir knight!' commanded Prospero, with a wave of the wand. Slowly the figure emerged from the draperies, and finally there in shining ghostly robes stood the tall figure of the departed knight, a red sash about his body suggesting he had met a bloody end. The figure provoked gasps from the audience, whether of fear or expectation I could not be sure.

'Are you ready to answer our questions?' asked Prospero.

The knight bowed his head.

'Then tap once upon the door for yes, and twice for no,' said Prospero.

There was another bow of the head. Then the glowing knight stepped into the cabinet and the door was closed.

'This noble knight protects us,' said Prospero to the audience. 'Rest assured that no bad spirits can enter this place. Ask him what you will, and he will answer.'

There was a moment of silence, then one of the gentlemen in the audience whispered to the lady beside him. She coughed and asked, 'Is the spirit of my grandmother residing in heaven?'

Unsurprisingly, there was a single firm tap on the door.

'Is grandfather by her side?'

Another tap.

'Oh,' exclaimed the lady, 'how I wish I could hear her voice again!'

From within the cabinet a soft piping voice began to render a hymn, and the lady dissolved into sobs. She was comforted by her companion. 'She never sang like that when she was alive,' he commented.

'Ah, but she is one of the angels, now,' said Prospero.

'I wish to speak to the spirit of the late Mr Alexander Ashbury,' said Holmes in a loud voice.

Prospero was clearly startled by this demand. 'I — do not think that is possible,' he said.

There were two loud raps on the door.

'But Mr Ashbury is dead is he not?' asked Holmes. 'He must be in spirit.'

Before Prospero could answer, there was a storm of rapping from inside the cabinet.

'What does that mean?' demanded the other lady in the audience.

'It means,' said Prospero, 'that the spirit of the deceased has descended into realms from which it cannot be called. Neither should any attempt be made to call it. Sir, I beg you to withdraw your request.'

'Very well, I will do so,' said Holmes, 'but it is really very inconvenient. The man in question met an untimely end at the hand of another, and it would be of great benefit to society if the villain could be identified.'

'So it would, so it would,' said Prospero, unhappily.

'Might I then be permitted to converse with the unhappy spirit of Dr Peralta?' Holmes continued. 'I feel he has unfinished business in this world and must still haunt this place.'

'Peralta is silent!' said Prospero, who was becoming increasingly agitated. 'He has been silenced. There are things he cannot say, *must* not say!'

'Who is this Peralta?' asked the second lady of the gentleman beside her.

'He was a conjuror, I heard he came to a bad end,' said her companion.

'He was my friend,' cried Prospero. 'And he was blameless. Blameless! Yes! He is here! I can sense him here now, at last! Peralta! Speak to me!' Prospero dropped his wand, clutched his head and moaned aloud. 'Oh, the shame! The agony!' He clasped his throat. 'Unhand me! I cannot breathe!' His top hat tumbled to the floor.

There was a scuffling noise in the cabinet and the door flew open. The tall knight stepped out, and wobbled alarmingly. Then the upper part of his body fell forward, and he split in half across the middle. There was a shriek of terror from the sobbing lady, matched only by the yelps of horror from her companion, who rose and quickly conducted her from the room.

Prospero had fallen to his knees and his son and daughter, having thrown off their shining robes, went to comfort him. Holmes allowed them a little time, then he rose and turned up the gas lamp. In the light, what had seemed in the dark to be ethereally shining garments turned out to be swathes of greyish muslin with an acrid chemical smell.

'Well!' exclaimed the second gentleman, rising to his feet. 'This is nothing but a great fraud! We should be repaid at once.'

His companion clutched at his arm. 'No,' she said, 'the poor man is obviously distressed. Let us go.'

With a loud 'Harrumph!' the man acquiesced, and they both departed.

'Father,' said Orlando. 'These gents are Mr Holmes and Mr Stamford who I told you about. They want to help.'

'No-one can help,' moaned Fishwick. 'Peralta was murdered, and then Ashbury was murdered, and now their killer is coming for me!'

Holmes and I helped him to his feet and guided him to one of the chairs, where he was a picture of dejection. He looked about forty but much worn for his years, with thinning hair and deep creases about his eyes. 'Do you know who the killer is?' asked Holmes.

At this moment the curtains in the cabinet were torn aside and a large man wearing a grubby apron and smelling of stale beer rushed into the room. I saw that the cabinet door had not led to a broom cupboard at all, but to the rear stairs of the building.

'I've had some complaints about you, Fishwick!' said the man. 'Upsetting people and tricking them out of money! You and your brats can pack your things and go!'

Fishwick sighed. 'Yes, Mr Grundy,' he said.

'I want you out tonight! Without fail!' Grundy stormed away.

'Where are you living at present?' asked Holmes.

'In the attic here,' sighed Fishwick, miserably.

'Have you somewhere to go?'

'Mr Flowers told me about a room. I hope I have enough to secure it.'

The Fishwick children looked through the cup of coins, which did not appear well filled.

Holmes glanced at me, and we both dipped our hands into our pockets and gave what we could.

'Thank you, gentlemen,' said Fishwick gratefully. 'I have been trying to earn enough money to leave London and make a new start elsewhere. I fear I am in danger here.'

'From Peralta's killer?' asked Holmes. 'Do you know his identity?'

'Yes. He was a conjuror who killed a man on stage. He admitted his guilt and suffered only a minor sentence and is now free again, but he hides under another name. He does not want anyone to know who he is. But Peralta knew. He told me the man was in London. He was called Tourmalin.'

CHAPTER TWENTY-TWO

Following our discussion with Mr Fishwick, Holmes searched the newspapers for the report of the inquest into the death of Dr Peralta, which had taken place in early February.

MELANCHOLY DEATH OF MAGICIAN

Stanley Potter, who once worked as a magician under the name Dr Peralta, was found dead in a common lodging house last Wednesday. His last major tour of the theatres was some eight years ago, but since then his fame declined. More recently he was forced to beg in the street, performing some of the tricks that he had once displayed on stage. A post-mortem has been carried out and it appears that he had been under the influence of alcohol at the time of his death. The body revealed his considerable dependence on liquor.

The cause of death was unusual. Mr Potter appears to have wetted a silk handkerchief, one he used in his act, and wound it about his neck, tying it tightly in a knot. A common tablespoon had been employed as a garrotte. This and the shrinking of the silk fabric had so tightened it about his neck, that it led to his death. The surgeon who examined the body said it was unusual for someone to garrotte themselves but not impossible if the individual lay in such a position that the ligature could not loosen itself. He especially noted that the silk scarf was a property the deceased had once used in his failed career. The only other injuries on the body were bruises of varying ages. This was not an uncommon finding in a person who drank to excess and suffered frequent falls.

On the morning of his death Mr Potter had told his landlady that he was due to meet with a man who he hoped would offer him work. It is not known if this meeting took place, but it seems very probable that he did

not receive an offer of work and had become despondent as a result. The
inquest jury recorded a verdict of suicide.

'Holmes,' I said, putting down the paper, 'please reassure me
you will not be attempting any dangerous experiments.'

'I shall not be trying to see if it is possible to garrotte myself,
if that is what you mean,' he said. 'I will take the word of the
examining surgeon that it can be done. A man determined to
die knows no obstacles. But I have mentioned the case to
Sergeant Lestrade. He agrees with me that there may be more
to the death of Peralta than might appear. He will make some
enquiries and revert to me if he learns anything of note. One
thing I should mention; Fishwick's concerns about Tourmalin
are without foundation. I have compared the date of Peralta's
death with Mr and Mrs Goodgold's term of employment in
Edinburgh. Since Mr Goodgold is unable to grow wings and
fly back and forth between his twice-daily performances, I
think we can safely say he has a perfect alibi.'

Holmes had been reflecting on his recent conversation with
Inspector Knight, in particular Mr Tapper's comment to his
friend Mrs Harding that he expected to make a good sum of
money from some business in London. 'Of course, he might
have been exaggerating in order to win the lady's hand,' said
Holmes. 'But if there was some scheme which he hoped might
earn him a large sum, he had only one valuable thing to trade
— the secrets he had learned of Mr Maskelyne's conjuring.
And those secrets lie in the one place in the Egyptian Hall we
have not as yet been permitted to enter.'

Maskelyne's workshop, where he devised all his inventions,
was his special sanctum. The only persons allowed inside apart
from himself were Mr Cooke, and on occasion, Mr Tapper,

who had to be instructed on the practical application of certain devices. It was therefore a great honour when Holmes and I, on making a humble application, were permitted to enter. This was on the very strict understanding that we were not to divulge its secrets to another soul.

Even though so many years have passed since the events in question, I will of course continue to respect that promise. Others may have copied Mr Maskelyne's performances and even published their own answers to the mysteries, but I will not be of that number.

Suffice it to say that the workshop was a veritable Aladdin's cave of wonders. Here resided Psycho when his daily work was done, also his companion, Zoe, an automaton in the form of a little girl who sat on a high stool before an easel and drew pictures of celebrated persons. I saw the progress of work on the new wonder, Fanfare, a gentleman in a morning suit who played the cornet, and plans for another musical device, Labial, who would be master of the euphonium.

We were also shown the development of Maskelyne's advanced levitation apparatus, a novel concept in those days, which enabled quite substantial objects to soar effortlessly aloft, without the audience being able to see the means by which they did so. 'Was Mr Tapper involved in the operation of this effect?' asked Holmes.

'He was, and since his demise I have been looking for a trustworthy man of experience to take his place. Mr Cooke is hoping in time to place the levitations in the hands of Mr Bromley, and he is progressing well.'

One item of interest in the room was a new cabinet, which resembled a two-door wardrobe. It was secured by a padlocked chain passing through the handles.

'I have decided to revive the cabinet act which formed a feature of our earlier performances in Cheltenham,' said Maskelyne. 'It is a relatively simple device, but it produces a comic interlude which our audiences always found highly entertaining. The old cabinet is long gone, of course, but this one has improved features, and we will be able to do a great deal more than before. The costumes have also been renewed. If you would stand back, gentlemen, I will demonstrate.'

He took a bunch of keys from his pocket, from which he selected one, unlocked the padlock, slid the chain free, and threw open the cabinet doors. The interior of the cabinet was meant to resemble a village lock-up with a barred section within, where prisoners could be temporarily lodged. 'In our comedy a young sailor is arrested and placed inside, while his sweetheart pleads for his release. Then a witch arrives and casts a spell, the sailor vanishes, and a gorilla appears in his place. But that is only the beginning.' He chuckled. 'You will have to see it for yourselves in time. There are humorous interludes and songs, and I need hardly tell you that all ends happily. I recall being taken to task in the press by the unusual aspect of the gorilla, which was blessed with a tail. Some people have no sense of humour.' He closed the doors, secured the cabinet, and was walking away when we heard a rapping noise from within. 'Dear me, who can that be?' he exclaimed, and reopened the doors to reveal Mr Cooke, who stepped out, smiling at our surprise.

'Well done!' I exclaimed. 'I wish I knew how that was achieved.'

'Might I see inside?' asked Holmes.

'The secret is not to be revealed,' said Maskelyne, closing and locking the doors before we were tempted to look more closely.

'Are you not concerned that a spy might conceal himself in there?' I asked.

'As you can see, I take great care to avoid that eventuality,' said Maskelyne. 'But I would easily be able to identify anyone who had been able to gain entry to my workshop without permission by examining his boots.'

I looked down at my boots, wondering what he meant by this, but Holmes took his meaning and instead stared at the floor. He took out his glass, then lowered himself into a crouching position, and began an earnest study of what appeared to be fragments of wood chips, sawdust and general sweepings.

'Ah,' said Maskelyne. 'You have observed the state of the floor. I do not permit the char lady to sweep here. When necessary, I attend to that myself. There is a brush by the door you may use on the soles of your boots as you leave.'

Holmes took an envelope from his pocket and used his penknife to sweep into it a sample of the floor debris, then sealed it and put it in his pocket.

'What have you found?' I asked.

'That will be determined under the microscope,' said Holmes. 'Mr Maskelyne, can you advise me of where you purchase the materials for your work? I assume they are delivered here?'

'Yes, I can show you some invoices. They come to the front door after Mr Jennings has opened up. He puts them behind the box office counter and alerts me to the delivery. I inspect the materials and take them into the workshop.'

'Were there any deliveries in the days immediately preceding the death of Mr Tapper?'

'Yes, there was one, about two or three days before.' Maskelyne went to his desk where there were a number of portfolios and examined a folder of papers. 'Yes, here it is.' Holmes was allowed to see the papers and made some notes. We thanked our host and left him to his work. Holmes had that look on his face when he is on the trail of answers but cannot say more until he is certain.

CHAPTER TWENTY-THREE

Holmes returned to the laboratory to examine the material he had collected from the floor of Maskelyne's workshop, but his work had not yet been completed when he received a note from Inspector Knight. Ashbury's body had been released to his father and the funeral was to take place in Walthamstow the following morning. We travelled there by railway in the company of Inspector Knight and a constable.

'I like to look around at a funeral,' said Knight. 'See who is there. Family of course, but in a case of murder I wonder if one of those present might be the killer? Shedding false tears for the deceased. Doesn't fool a perceptive policeman, of course. In the case of Mr Ashbury, I may be spoiled for choice. Some might be there only to reassure themselves that he really is dead. A few will no doubt be looking for the opportunity to dance on his grave. Others might be having a word with the father about money they are owed.'

'What family do you expect?' asked Holmes.

'Just the father.'

We alighted at Hoe Street station. From there it was a short stroll to the square-towered parish church of St Mary's, where, Knight told us, the Ashburys had a family plot. Its galleries and benches provided seating for a large congregation, but few were present for the funeral of Alexander Ashbury.

Apart from ourselves the only attendees were Ashbury senior, and a small cluster of persons, all of whom appeared to know each other. I thought they were there to support the bereaved father in his grief rather than mourn the deceased. Inspector Knight told us that they were the staff and regular customers of the Fallow Deer public house. No client of the deceased's business, no friend if he had had any, had come to remember him.

After the usual opening words from the clergyman, who was well practised at speaking of a man he had never met, Ashbury's father addressed us. Despite his age he was, unlike his son, strong on his feet, with a clear voice.

'I want to say a few words about my boy,' he began. 'Alexander was born in Chingford, upstairs in the Fallow Deer. He was never sure what he wanted to do with his life, but the one thing he knew from a very early age was that he didn't want to run a public house. Oh, he worked behind the bar when he was young, but he never took to it. I was sorry about that as I had hoped he would take over from me as licensee one day. He felt sure his future lay in London, and he spent a great deal of time there. About fifteen years ago he saw a performance at the theatre, a magician — a man long forgotten now, Herr Leonid Blume. That was when everything changed for him. Alexander talked of nothing else. He wanted to be like Blume; he wanted to *be* Blume. Next thing I knew, he had arranged to meet the man and said he wanted to be his assistant and learn from him. Blume was somewhat advanced in years, and he needed a younger man to carry his bags and arrange travel and whatever else an assistant does. Alexander went on tour with Herr Blume: after London, there was Paris, Vienna, they travelled all over Europe. I didn't see him again for three years.

'When my son came back, he was not the same. Blume had died abroad; he had been killed in an accident on stage. A dangerous trick that failed. Alexander had had to finalise all his affairs. Then he became ill from the strain of it all — pneumonia. It brought him close to death and he took six months to recover. You might have read in the newspapers that the doctor who spoke at the inquest said he had found an old wound in the chest and thought he might have been stabbed. Now, I am not a doctor, but it seems to me that it was nothing but an old scar from the pneumonia. Alexander never told me he had been stabbed. But whatever it was, it had weakened him, and he knew he would never be a magician, never be robust enough to tour the world. But he still had that love for the stage, and he had learned so much about it during his time with Herr Blume. That was when he started his business as a promoter of other acts.' He sighed. 'I'm not saying he was the best. But it was what he wanted to do — it meant a lot to him. That is all I can say.'

After the hymns had been sung, we filed out to the graveside. Once the interment was done, we were told that Ashbury had arranged for carriages to the public house so we could drink to the deceased.

The Fallow Deer was one of those large, sprawling buildings dating from the days before the railways, but still with an antique charm. One could imagine less sombre days greeting the arrival of a coachload of merry Pickwickians. We sat at a scrubbed wooden table laden with beer, cold beef, bread, butter and pickles, cheese and pastries. Inspector Knight introduced us to Ashbury senior, who joined us.

'Mr Ashbury, I am sorry to have to ask you some further questions at this time, but we are hoping to learn something to enable us to find the person responsible for your son's death,' said Knight.

'Are you sure it wasn't an accident?' asked Ashbury senior plaintively.

'Yes, we are quite sure.'

'Do you happen to know if your son ever owned a gun?' asked Holmes.

'No, never,' replied Ashbury firmly. 'Did you know that Herr Blume died after being shot with his own gun? When Alexander told me about Herr Blume's act, catching a bullet in his mouth, I was horrified. He tried to reassure me it was not as dangerous as it appeared, it was just a trick. After what happened, however, he would have nothing to do with guns. He had found that even the most experienced man could make a fatal mistake.'

'Did he ever mention anything to you that might have resulted in this attack?'

'It's a strange business, conjuring,' said the old man, regretfully. 'Rivalry, jealousy… Buying and selling and stealing secrets. Who knows what might have happened? I hardly knew any of these people so could not say who might have had a grudge.'

'When did you last see your son? Was he at all nervous?'

'No, quite the reverse. He came to see me about three weeks ago and he was very cheerful; he said he could see his way to doing much better in future. Mind you, he had to borrow a few pounds from me, but he said he would pay it back.'

'Did he say what kind of business he thought would do well for him?' asked Holmes. 'A new act to promote, perhaps?'

'No, it wasn't that, not a person; it was something to do with conjuring. Something all the magicians wanted to be able to do and couldn't, and he thought he could get the secret.'

'I don't suppose he told you what that secret might be?' said Knight.

'He said to me, "Supposing you could see a man fly through the air, lift himself off the stage, and float over the heads of the audience, and there was nothing to hold him up? What would you think?" And I said it would be a miracle and he just laughed.'

Holmes was thoughtful on the return journey. At last, he said, 'I believe Ashbury lied to his father about having pneumonia. At least I believe that if he did develop a disorder of the lung, it was as a result of the stab wound found at the post-mortem, which he must have suffered when he was touring abroad with Herr Blume. This means there have been two attacks upon his person, one with some unknown implement, which nearly proved fatal, and one with a gun. Can they be connected? Mr Maskelyne mentioned Herr Blume to us when we were discussing dangerous acts. I shall see if he can tell me anything more.'

'And what was this secret about flying through the air?' asked Knight.

'Maskelyne has created a new means of effecting a levitation effect on stage,' explained Holmes. 'One in which even large apparatus can take flight, and the means of support is completely invisible to the eye. It is the envy of his rivals. I think Ashbury must have been hoping to lay his hands on it.'

'But who knew the secret?'

'As far as I am aware, only three persons: Mr Maskelyne, his partner Mr Cooke, and the trusted assistant, Mr Tapper.'

CHAPTER TWENTY-FOUR

Once we were able to secure an interview with Mr Maskelyne, which took place as he enjoyed a brief repast between the matinee and the evening performances, Holmes told him of the funeral we had just attended and what we had learned about the deceased.

'Ashbury's father said that his son once worked as an assistant to Herr Leonid Blume. That magician was killed while performing the bullet catch, which led to Ashbury's horror of guns. I recalled your mentioning to me a Herr Blume who died in that way. That must have been the same man.'

'I expect so,' said Maskelyne. 'There are families of magicians, of course, and acts are passed down from father to son, but I do not know of another of that name.'

'Did you ever see Herr Blume perform?'

'As a matter of fact I did, when he toured England last. That would have been some fifteen years ago. He was then about sixty-five. In fair health, but a little stiff about the knees, so I could well imagine he might have required a younger man to assist him.'

'What was you impression of him?'

Maskelyne smiled at the memory. 'I thought him polished and experienced. The movements of his hands were refined and beautifully elegant. He presented his material most attractively to the audience. I was then just learning my art, and he inspired me to do better. In fact, I was shocked and surprised when I learned of his death and the suggestion that it was a result of carelessness.'

'Where did this take place?'

'In Paris, I believe.' He paused. 'I was once told Blume had rivals — enemies, and you know how they can twist the truth. Some of them spread the rumour that he had not been shot at all. It was said to be a trick so he could disappear, to avoid being arrested for nameless offences, an accusation which shocked everyone who knew him. But I have it on good authority that he really was shot and was carried from the stage in a very dangerous state. He has not been seen since, and his memory has faded into obscurity.'

'Perhaps Blume made a mistake due to failing eyesight,' I suggested.

'Or the error was made by his assistant,' said Holmes. 'If it *was* an error. I shall ask Inspector Knight if he can request information regarding the incident from the Paris police.'

Maskelyne had no more to tell us, and Holmes returned to the laboratory.

The following morning, I was emerging from a lecture when Holmes came to see me, and we retired to a coffee house to talk. 'I have received a note from Lestrade,' he said. 'He was not involved in the investigation into Peralta's death, but he has found that there was a suggestion at the time that he had received a visit from a lady shortly before, and that this might have increased his melancholy. He is hoping to discover more.'

'That was not mentioned at the inquest,' I said.

'Lestrade thinks that there was some evidence which, while not proof of any crime, was not made public, in case further information became available which might lead to a revised verdict.'

'Did you discover anything in the dust on the workshop floor?' I asked.

'I did indeed,' said Holmes, and I need to make further enquiries to determine what it means.'

'Oh?'

'Let us consider once more the unusual death of Mr Thomas Tapper,' said Holmes. 'Which may or may not have been as a result of criminality. We know that Tapper must have died at some time after ten o'clock. The only other persons known to have been in the building after the audience and the performers had departed, were Mr Maskelyne and Mr Bromley. I am not aware that either had a motive to kill Tapper. Either might have tied him up as a prank. I cannot imagine Mr Maskelyne panicking and concealing an accidental death. And Bromley? If he was responsible I feel sure he would have confessed to his uncle by now.

'We have discussed the possibility that a person unknown who attended the performance, had concealed themselves on the premises, and emerged to confront Mr Tapper. Either that or the unknown person had an arrangement to meet Tapper and was admitted by him. We know that Tapper was in possession of a secret which was valued by Mr Ashbury, a secret he had told his father he hoped to acquire. Ashbury did not want Tapper dead, of course; he wanted him alive and talking. He might have promised someone a generous payment for that secret, if only Tapper could be persuaded to talk.

'Tapper had one weakness — he thought he could perform the rope escape, which was the centre of Mr Maskelyne and Mr Cooke's anti-spiritual séance exposing the Davenports' fraud. And I am sure he could, using the same rope, a smooth thick manila, easy to loosen and slip out of. But he laid himself open to being trapped. Asked to demonstrate his skill, someone tied him with the rough, thin jute rope, a rope which he could not loosen however hard he tried. Perhaps threats were made, threats to leave him there all night unless he gave up his secrets, the secrets which were behind the locked door of Mr

Maskelyne's workshop. But it seems that Tapper did not give up the secrets. He panicked and struggled, and his weak heart stopped, and he died.

'There was only one clue in the cabinet to suggest that another person had been present, the fibres of jute rope. This rope was untied and removed, and replaced with the manila, in the hope that it would seem that Tapper had been practising the trick alone.

'This unknown person must have arrived with the intention of threatening Tapper, bringing with him the rough rope he knew he would need. He left taking it with him. It is a very promising theory which fits all the facts in my possession thus far. Importantly, jute rope is not used or stored in the Egyptian Hall. No trace of it has been found there.' Holmes paused. 'Until now.'

I was about to ask where, when I realised that I knew.

'Mr Maskelyne's workshop!' I declared.

'Indeed. When we were shown around the workshop, I saw small threads amongst the dust on the floor which appeared to the eye to be jute. I examined them under the microscope, and it was the same material as the rope which had tied Mr Tapper. But how did it enter the hall? The answer was simple. It is a type of rope used to secure packages. This morning, my enquiries established that one of the companies which delivered materials to the hall used just this kind of rope.

'I fear, however,' Holmes continued, 'that this discovery does not greatly narrow the field of suspects. It is possible that Tapper might have known and trusted one of the delivery men and been willing to admit him to the hall after hours. The next step will be to speak to Mr Jennings and discover how packages were received and how the rope that bound them was disposed of.'

There was a gleam in Holmes's eyes which I recognised. It indicated that the hunt was on, and I was happy to accompany him.

The box office was busy as usual, but a quick word with Mr Jennings ensured that we would be able to speak to him when he closed it briefly during the luncheon hour. He was very obliging and invited us into his working space behind the shutters. We saw a clean and uncluttered space, where a set of pigeonholes on the far wall held the stock of tickets. There was a brass till for money, a small safe which held the books of account, a stout leather bag for transporting the daily takings to the bank, and neat piles of leaflets advertising current and future attractions. A small metal wastebin held only some torn leaflets, and used envelopes, and the floor had been well swept with a hand brush.

'Packages arriving for Mr Maskelyne are delivered here,' Mr Jennings confirmed. 'I do not take them to Mr Maskelyne directly, they are passed to me, and I keep them behind the counter until he comes to collect them. There is not usually long to wait, as he knows when something is expected and comes to check with me frequently.'

'Do these packages come wrapped in paper and tied with thin rope or string?'

'Many of them are, yes.'

'Who removes the packaging? How is it deposed of?'

'Mr Maskelyne cuts them open to see what is inside, then he takes the contents into his workshop. He passes the paper and string to me to dispose of. I have a waste receptacle here, as you see.' Jennings indicated the wastebin.

'How often is that emptied?'

'Every day — it is the last thing done before I leave for the bank.'

'You dispose of the materials yourself?'

'No, Mr Tapper used to do that and after he died, I ask Peter.'

'Wrapping paper and rope or string are useful things to keep in case they are needed,' Holmes observed. 'Many people like to retain some for their own use.'

'That is true, but in a theatre, it does not do to leave flammable materials around. Gentlemen can be very careless with their cigars.'

'Jute is highly flammable, is it not?'

'It is. I suppose the parcel string might have been composed of jute. Paper and string are as good as any kindling.'

'Has anyone here ever asked you for some for their own use?'

'Not that I can recall.'

'The position of the wastebin; could someone have leaned over the counter and helped himself?'

'I suppose that might have been possible, although I have never seen anyone do so.'

That was all we were to learn from Mr Jennings, and he returned to his duties.

'Now we know why the jute fibres were on the workshop floor,' I said.

'And any threads of jute which might have fallen to the floor in the foyer were swept up by the char lady or Mr Bromley, while Mr Jennings keeps his own little area clean,' added Holmes. 'Unless I can uncover something further, I cannot arrive at a conclusion.'

On his return to Barts, Holmes's spirits were lifted somewhat by the arrival of Inspector Knight, and we retired to the chemistry laboratory to talk.

'I have had a letter from the police force in Paris,' said Knight. 'There was a lot more to the late Herr Blume than met the eye. His real name was Leonid Blumenthal, and when he was touring Paris in May 1866 he was questioned by the police concerning allegations made against him by young ladies — mainly the use of insulting language. He denied the allegations and as there was no actual evidence, and no witnesses to his behaviour, he was not charged. The police did keep an eye on him, however. In view of the number of accusations by ladies who did not know each other, and had nothing to gain by making such statements, suspicions remained. It was thought possible that there might have been more serious matters which could lead to criminal charges, and the ladies concerned too afraid or ashamed to speak out.'

'Had there been similar accusations previously?' asked Holmes.

'Not that anyone has reported. His friends said he had always been of good character. But he was a magician — good at concealing the truth.'

'I have been told that there were rumours about him, but it was suggested that these were fabricated by jealous rivals,' said Holmes.

'There might have been some truth in them after all,' said Knight. 'But before anything further could be discovered, he died by his own bullet in the following month.'

'Did the police look into that?'

'No, it was thought to be an accident. There were enough witnesses.'

'Mr Maskelyne has observed to me that he was surprised to learn of Blume making such a mistake. He had seen him perform and thought very highly of his skills as a conjurer.'

'That might have been true once, but Blume had been in poor health not long before he died. He had been obliged to cancel all his engagements in Vienna some four months before he came to Paris, due to illness.'

'Do you know the nature of his illness?'

'It was not specified. Perhaps it was some brain disease. That might account for what happened.'

'His enemies have also suggested that he was not shot at all; that it was a trick to avoid arrest. Have you seen a report of the shooting?'

'I was told he had loaded the gun himself and asked a volunteer from the audience to shoot him, saying that it was quite safe to do so. The man fired the gun and Blume fell, bleeding from a wound in the chest, and crying out that he had been shot. He was still alive when carried from the stage and a doctor was called. The next day a newspaper reported that his life was despaired of, and a few days later we were told that he had died, and his body would be taken to the city of his birth for burial.'

'That city being?'

'Not named.'

Holmes grunted in frustration. 'At least I now have the year and month for the incident, which will make my further enquiries much simpler. In the meantime, Inspector, I would like you to make some enquiries in Vienna to see if we can arrive at the nature of Herr Blume's illness there. I suggest you use both his stage name and birth name.'

'What do you think this illness might have been?'

'I can't say for certain,' said Holmes grimly, 'but I have a very strong suspicion.'

As Knight made a record in his notebook, Holmes told him of his discovery of the jute fibres.

'My attention has always been on the individuals working at the Egyptian Hall, the people who knew Tapper and had the best motive to want to threaten him,' said Knight. 'This discovery strengthens my case. I think I shall go back and question them all again, it might jog a few memories.'

Holmes continued his research at the British Museum Library, and he later shared his findings with me. The English newspapers carried only brief and often contradictory accounts of the death of Herr Blume; fortunately, the Paris journals were more informative. One included a detailed description by an eyewitness. Herr Blume, after performing before the clientele of all the major hotels in Paris, was appearing at the Cirque Napoléon. He had been in high spirits, performing with confidence and verve. The observer, knowing that the conjuror had been ill some weeks previously, commented that he appeared to have made a full recovery. The programme began with a number of simple tricks using a magic wand to produce flags and ribbons from a hat, and other similar and well-known effects. When it came to loading the gun, Blume, with a humorous flourish, had used the wand as a ramrod. The wand appeared to have stuck a little and he had to shake it from side to side to pull it out, but all had seemed well until the gun was fired and he fell, with blood on his shirt front.

'He could have faked the shooting,' I said. 'He claps a hand to his chest as the gun fires, releasing a phial of stage blood under his shirt, and is carried from the stage before he can be examined. Then he sends out an announcement of his death.

He changes his name and appearance and starts a new career somewhere where he will not be recognised. That business with the wand might have been part of the trick.'

'And Herr Blume disappears,' said Holmes. 'But I think I know exactly where he is.'

'Where?' I exclaimed.

'Once I have heard from Inspector Knight, I will be certain. You must be patient, Stamford.'

I am a patient man, but sometimes Holmes did try my patience.

CHAPTER TWENTY-FIVE

I had been hoping that Mr Fishwick would use his income as Prospero and the additional coins that Holmes and I had given him to secure some safe place for himself and his children and find a means of making an honest income. Unfortunately, he disappointed us. On the Tuesday following the disastrous séance I received a message from Holmes. It consisted of a brief note and a crudely printed leaflet.

The only true exponent of the daring feats of Scott, the famous American diver!
Challenge to the World! 100gns wager!
Ariel, the British champion diver, will at 2pm on Tuesday next perform the famous rope trick in which he dances on air, before diving 40 feet into the water from Waterloo Bridge.

Holmes's note read: *Meet me outside Somerset House 1pm. Police have already been informed.*

When I arrived, a large and expectant crowd had already gathered along Strand, the numbers moving along in orderly fashion south onto Waterloo Bridge. Fortunately, there was something of a carnival atmosphere, and everything was proceeding under the watchful eyes of a force of constables. My only fear was the speed at which a peaceful crowd fuelled by disappointment could be transformed into a rioting mob. I was glad that Holmes had designated a meeting place, otherwise it might have delayed finding him. 'What is this about?' I asked.

'I fear that the funds we supplied to Mr Fishwick for the housing and feeding of his family have been employed to advertise this demonstration,' he said.

'You are sure this Ariel is he?' I asked.

'I was sent the advertisement by Mr Flowers. And Ariel is the spirit servant of Shakespeare's Prospero,' he said. 'Come and see what he has done.' We joined the little procession approaching the bridge. The roadway was littered with discarded leaflets, and scraps of greasy paper which had once held buns and sausages.

Above the central arch of the bridge, where one of its row of tall gas lamps stood, was a curious construction of wooden scaffolding poles standing in the roadway, all roughly lashed together. Two poles were standing vertically several feet apart, each tied to a pillar of the balustrade. They were connected by two horizontal poles placed between them, one about three feet from the top of the balustrade, the other a further five feet above it. Two boatmen who must have been hired for the occasion stood guard, one on either side of this ramshackle edifice, to stop members of the crowd from climbing up it.

'Surely he is not going to jump from so high up?' I said, aghast. 'It is dangerous enough to jump off the bridge as it is.'

'Most individuals who survive such falls are women,' said Holmes. 'They are usually bent on self-destruction. Their skirts slow the fall, and the wearer is buoyed up long enough to be rescued. A professional diver who is experienced may know a technique to ensure his safety, but I am not sure that Mr Fishwick has ever done this before. I don't even know if he can swim. The whole enterprise smacks of desperation.'

'Will the police not stop him?' I looked about me. The constables were mainly engaged in keeping the peace and preventing daring youths from clambering onto the balustrade for a better view.

'It does not appear at present that anything being advertised is against the law,' said Holmes.

'What does he hope to gain? Has he taken out wagers?'

'See there,' said Holmes, pointing to where two small but familiar figures were marching up and down the lines of onlookers. Orlando and Jessica Fishwick, tin boxes suspended from around their necks with string, were rattling coins and calling out for donations.

'At least he is intending to jump from the middle point of the arch,' I said. 'He will land in the water and not on the stone supports. There are some boats out there so he may be saved.'

'And there he is,' said Holmes, as Mr Fishwick came into view, a slight figure amongst the burly boatmen. He was cheerfully inspecting the apparatus, nodding in a satisfied manner. He was carrying a coil of rope over one arm, its immediate purpose being not apparent.

'I can see Mr and Mrs Flowers,' said Holmes. 'They may be able to tell us more.'

We hurried through the milling throng to where Mr Flowers and his wife, both of whom carried collection boxes, were parading behind the Fishwick children, and keeping a watchful eye on them. Crowds of people were still arriving, and a large crush was in the process of being formed.

'Oh, Mr Holmes,' exclaimed Mrs Flowers, 'I am so glad you are here. We did our best to persuade Mr Fishwick not to go ahead with his stunt, but he said he had promised, and asked us to come and look after the children while he performed. We couldn't say no.'

'Has he done anything like this before?' I asked.

'No, it's something he read about, and he got it into his head that he could make money for the children.'

'I tried to dissuade him, but he wouldn't listen,' said Mr Flowers.

'He could be badly injured or even die,' I said.

We all glanced towards Mr Fishwick. Still with the rope coiled about one arm, he clambered up onto the balustrade, then stepped off it to stand on the lower rail. The onlookers cheered, and he smiled and waved at them.

'Is that a safety rope?' I asked. 'Will he tie himself to one of the poles?'

'My father saw the American diver, Scott, all those years ago,' said Mr Flowers, gloomily. 'He used to swing on the rope before he dived in.'

Mr Fishwick was reaching up to tie one end of the rope to the upper pole. The other end we now saw was in a very recognisable shape — a hangman's noose.

'When you say "swing" —' I began, but was cut off as Holmes, his face pale with the horrid realisation of Fishwick's intentions, seized me by the arm and set off at a run, pulling me behind him.

We rushed along the road towards the bridge, which was already lined three deep with crowds and an insufficient number of policemen doing their best to keep order. Before we could approach the scaffold, one of the boatmen stepped in our way. He was a large fellow, with thick arms and a face like an ox. 'Now then, no-one is allowed any closer. Orders of Mr Ariel.'

Holmes tried to dash past, but the width of the boatman impeded him and despite my friend's pleas to be allowed to prevent a disaster, there was a struggle. There was no time for an extended fight, and even with Holmes's wrestling skills he was bound to lose. The other boatman came and stood in my way, his size and expression being more than sufficient to prevent me from tackling him.

'Look!' I shouted at the man, pointing up at Oliver Fishwick. 'Look what he is going to do! We must stop him!'

Fishwick, having secured one end of the rope, now placed the noose about his neck. He stood on the lower pole and extended his arms like a diver about to make a plunge. There were anxious gasps from the crowd, and the boatmen, turning to look, uttered imprecations I will not record here, as they realised what was about to happen. There was no more fighting, and they and Holmes dashed forward to try and stop the madness. But they were too late.

Mr Fishwick took flight.

There was no drop on the rope, he simply swung out from his perch, and swung back again, his full weight supported by his neck. The crowd roared. In moments he was back in place, gasping a little, his life undoubtedly spared by the position of the knot under his chin, and his lean form.

Holmes reached the apparatus and began to climb up one side pole. 'Fishwick! Come down! You have done all you need to do; now you must stop while you can!'

'Three times!' shouted Fishwick. 'Three is the charm, and then I dive in!' To our horror, he swung out a second time, and such was the sway on the apparatus, that Holmes had to stop and hold on for dear life so as not to be pitched into the Thames forty feet below. Fishwick once more regained his position, although I could see he was tiring, and pulled at the noose around his neck to make it easier. As he rested, and Holmes continued his ascent, I decided to try my luck at reaching Fishwick from the other side of the scaffold. I do not have the length of leg or the reach of Holmes, but as a sportsman, and then aged twenty-four, I was at the peak of my bodily fitness. I began to climb.

Holmes had by now stepped onto the lower crosswise pole and began to edge along it towards Fishwick, his hands grasping the upper pole. It was becoming apparent that the structure, while strong enough for one slender man, was being seriously challenged to support the weight of three, and it began to tremble alarmingly. As I reached the first level, I felt it shudder and then it lurched forward, and for several moments it leaned over the balustrade, straining at the ropes attaching it, threatening to break apart and pitch us all into the murky water. My feet slipped from the lower crosswise pole, and I was left holding onto the upper one with both hands.

Dangling over the Thames, I closed my eyes and prayed. With no-one near enough to bring me to safety, I determined to hold on for as long as I could. Then, quite suddenly and unexpectedly, everything righted itself. Looking down, I saw the two muscular boatmen heaving the whole contraption back to the vertical. They did not look like blessed angels, but I was in no position to complain. To my great relief, my feet found the lower pole once more, and I lodged there, fighting for breath, my shoulders burning with the effort. Holmes, I was pleased to see, was also safe.

'Three!' cried Fishwick, launching himself once more from the scaffold, but this time, something had changed. The loosened rope slipped as he jumped, and the knot was now at the back of his neck. He gasped, and while he swung back, he was unable to gain his footing on the pole, and remained suspended, his body twitching.

Moments later, Holmes reached him. He wrapped an arm about the man's body, lifting him to release the tightness of the noose, his other hand grasping the upper pole, supporting the weight of them both. 'Stamford!' he called, but I was already moving along the lower pole, sliding my feet towards him, and was able on reaching Holmes and his burden to support myself by passing one arm over the top pole, enabling me to use both hands to loosen the rope sufficiently to lift the noose over Fishwick's head. There was cheering from the onlookers as the rope swung free.

Some constables had assembled below, not daring to try and ascend in case their weight caused the whole structure to collapse. We were able to hand the man down into their care before we descended to the bridge, and Fishwick was gently laid upon the ground.

'We should summon a surgeon?' asked a constable.

I had shortly before this event received my examination results, and for the first time in my life I was able to declare, 'I am a surgeon.'

The words had an almost instantaneous effect. The constables stood aside and I examined Fishwick, who was breathing, although in some distress. Fortunately, his features showed no serious signs of strangulation, and his pulse was racing but strong. His neck was scraped and bruised, but I could detect no damage to any vital structures beneath. 'I think the man will live,' I said. His life had undoubtedly been saved by the fact that he had not been subjected to a drop, which would have broken his spine, and had been suspended for only a few moments.

Fishwick opened his eyes. 'I haven't done the dive yet,' he whispered.

'Nor shall you,' I replied. 'I am going to take you to hospital where you may be properly examined and any injuries dressed.' I looked up at the constables. 'Kindly summon a carriage to transport my patient.' One of the constables scurried away to do my bidding. I was beginning to realise that my new position in life had some profound advantages.

I wasn't sure what Holmes might think of this development. He had left my side to speak to the police, who were holding back the crowd, and returned bringing with him Mr and Mrs Flowers and the Fishwick children. Fishwick was making efforts to sit up and complete his inadvisable performance, but on desperate appeals from both his friends and family, was eventually persuaded not to make a further attempt.

The crowds, although cheated of the excitement of a dive, had no reason to complain of any lack of entertainment, and once the carriage arrived to take Mr Fishwick to Barts, accompanied by Holmes and I, the police oversaw an orderly dispersal to their homes.

'Mr and Mrs Flowers have the children safely in their charge,' said Holmes, reassuringly. 'And I have been given to understand that there has been a most satisfactory monetary collection.'

'I wanted to do what I could for them,' croaked Fishwick. 'I had to, in case Tourmalin came for me.'

'I am not sure that Tourmalin is the dangerous fellow you imagine him to be,' said Holmes.

'You know him?' asked Fishwick anxiously.

'I have encountered him. And I do not believe he is guilty of any negligence in the case of the unfortunate death of Mr Winstone. Had your friend Peralta been alive, he might have been able to furnish me with his account of the affair. But even that assurance might not have been sufficient to exonerate Tourmalin. And since he has accepted blame, I doubt that the court's verdict can be reversed. He would, however, be most grateful to know the truth.'

'Tourmalin did not kill Peralta?'

'No. He was not in London at the time of Peralta's death.'

Fishwick absorbed this information. 'Peralta had something. From when Winstone was killed.'

'I am not aware that anything of importance was found amongst his possessions,' said Holmes.

Fishwick coughed painfully. 'That was because he gave it to me.'

CHAPTER TWENTY-SIX

Mr Fishwick was struggling to speak, and I had to advise him to rest his voice as much as possible, despite Holmes's impatience to know more.

Happily, an examination carried out at the hospital showed that Fishwick had suffered no serious injury from his adventure. The minor abrasions were treated, and soothing medicines supplied to be carefully administered.

Fishwick and his children were lodging in one corner of the rooms occupied by Mr and Mrs Flowers. It was a temporary arrangement, which suited no-one, but was tolerated by all. We brought him there to be reunited with his family and I supplied instructions as to how much medicine he should take and what food and drink he was to be allowed. Jessica at once appointed herself head nurse, and took charge of her father, her supervision involving delivering serious instructions that he should rest as much as possible and was not to speak unless necessary.

It was agreed that we would return once a further interview was permitted.

We could not avoid noticing an unusual presence in the room — Osric. The puppet and its box were in the process of being repaired, and Mr and Mrs Flowers, having taken possession of it, were intending to create a comical sketch around its supposed adventures. Orlando demonstrated to us how he used to curl his body inside the box to operate Osric. Although he had grown a little since he first took the stage with Mr Fiz, he declared that the damage to the box had expanded its sides and made it an easier fit than before. He suggested that Jessica could take his place, an idea she treated with disdain.

'No-one is going inside the box,' said Mrs Flowers firmly. 'You can stand behind it, Orlando, and if you draped yourself in a black cloth which covers your face and hands, no-one would see you, and you could work it with sticks if you like. It is a very old and simple device, but none the less effective for that.'

Sergeant Lestrade arranged a meeting with us in a suitable hostelry, eager to hear the whole story of the dramatic rescue of Mr Fishwick. 'I trust that he will not be prosecuted for any misdemeanour he may have committed?' said Holmes.

'I think the police have taken the view that he has suffered enough on this occasion,' said Lestrade. 'But should he attempt such an unwise action again, we will take him into custody for his own safety.'

'I shall make sure he is aware of this,' said Holmes. 'He would not wish to be parted from his children.'

'I have one piece of news for you,' added Lestrade. 'The reason why it was believed that Peralta had received a lady visitor shortly before his death. We like to keep possible clues close so only the police and the criminal will know of them. In this case we found a fragment of a feather in Peralta's room. It was a dyed feather of the sort ladies wear in their hats.'

'Might I suggest,' said Holmes, 'that you compare it with the feathers worn by the late Mr Ashbury in his Tyrolean hat?'

Lestrade looked astonished, then he leaped to his feet. 'You may have something there, Mr Holmes. I will see to it and let you know!' He hurried away.

'I am coming to the conclusion that whoever ended Mr Ashbury's life was a benefactor to society,' said Holmes. 'I would be sorry to see that individual punished.'

The following day we received a note to inform us that Mr Fishwick was greatly improved and wished to speak to us.

Fortified by a warm drink sweetened with honey, he sat at a table and greeted us. His voice was a little hoarse, but he was obviously better both in health and spirits. He reassured us that he would never again undertake such a hazardous enterprise. The Scott exhibition of mock hanging was, he now realised, too dangerous. He had heard of Monsieur Blondin crossing a tightrope on a velocipede, but had decided not to attempt it as he was unable to afford such a machine, or ride one without falling off. It had been decided that he and the children would join forces with Mr and Mrs Flowers and develop a programme of entertainment to display all their talents.

'Tell me about your friend Peralta,' said Holmes. 'His account of what happened on the night Mr Winstone was killed.'

'Peralta was not at fault,' said Fishwick. 'Not really. He never meant to hurt anyone. But he was afraid that he would be blamed for what happened if he spoke out. He and Tourmalin were rivals, they did similar acts, but Tourmalin drew greater crowds. Ashbury made it his business to find out where Tourmalin was due to appear and put in Peralta first. Then Tourmalin outdid Peralta by introducing the bullet catch spectacle. Peralta could not perform it, and Ashbury had a horror of such things. Did you know he once assisted Herr Blume, who was killed performing it in Paris?

'Ashbury went to see Tourmalin and saw how he worked the business. He thought if he could make the trick fail, and Tourmalin looked foolish on stage, he could write to all the newspapers denouncing him as a charlatan. He created a bullet for that purpose. I think he learned something of those things when he worked for Herr Blume. I don't know, and neither did Peralta, what it was supposed to do. Ashbury told Peralta to go and see Tourmalin, and volunteer to load the gun for the shot he was supposed to catch. When he was asked to select a bullet from the box, he should take one, palm it, and substitute the one he was given. It was that charge, the one made by Ashbury, which exploded and killed Mr Winstone.

'Peralta was shocked, terrified. He ran from the theatre. He knew that had Winstone not volunteered to fire the gun, he would have been asked to do it, and might have died instead, or been horribly injured. Soon afterwards he broke from Ashbury, who warned him that if he breathed a word of what happened it would be the worse for him.'

'You said Peralta gave you something,' said Holmes.

'Yes. It was some days later that Peralta looked in his coat pocket and realised that he still had the bullet, the one he had taken from Tourmalin's box. Ashbury had asked him for it, but he was so distracted he could not remember what he had done with it and said he had thrown it away. He examined it and saw that there was a mark scratched on it, a mark Tourmalin must have used to identify his bullets.'

'I have been told that there were two shots fired in the act,' said Holmes. 'The first one was a live round fired by Tourmalin at a target to convince the audience that his bullets were real. I have not been told exactly how it was done, but my theory is that Tourmalin started with a box of bullets which were all his specially prepared ones. He took one from the box and loaded the gun, but as he did so he substituted a live round and fired at the target. The volunteer then took a bullet from the same box, so it will always have had two removed at that point. Peralta had to have retained the one he took. He could not simply make a change or the numbers remaining in the box would have been wrong, and a substitution would have been suspected. At least, had anyone taken the trouble to count.'

Fishwick pulled a small chip box from his pocket and opened it, spilling the bullet onto the table.

'May I examine it?' asked Holmes.

'You may.'

Holmes spent several minutes gazing at the bullet through his glass, and at last he nodded. 'Yes, I see the mark, it is very distinct. Would you permit me to keep hold of it? The one that exploded was too damaged to provide any identification.'

'I would be most relieved to see it in safe hands. What will happen now?'

'I will consider what to do. Peralta and Ashbury are both beyond the law. Do you still believe Peralta was murdered?'

'I do. I had thought it was by Tourmalin, but now I think it was Ashbury's work, to silence him.'

'I agree. Peralta knew that Ashbury was to blame for the death of Mr Winstone. He had kept the secret out of fear, but I think his financial plight was so desperate that he risked demanding money from Ashbury for his silence. He may even have offered to provide this marked bullet for a price. As a result, Ashbury killed him.'

We were just considering this when a police sergeant and a constable arrived at the lodging house and demanded admission.

'Mr Fishwick? You have been a hard man to find.'

Fishwick looked confused. 'What do you want of me?'

'If you would like to accompany us to the station we would like to ask you some further questions regarding the murder of Mr Alexander Ashbury.'

CHAPTER TWENTY-SEVEN

'I have learned,' said Holmes the following day, 'that the police have been examining the alibis of all those who might have had a motive to kill Ashbury. They think that Mr Fishwick had enough time to travel from where he was to perform his séance that evening, to Ashbury's lodging house, carry out the murder and return without being missed. They have discounted the alibis provided by his children. There is now a Chief Inspector leading the case who is very eager to make an arrest. It really is stretching credulity. I hope they will admit failure and release Fishwick soon.'

We were in Holmes's dreadfully untidy rooms at the time, where, having been regaled with a modest supper, I was assisting him by pasting cuttings into a new commonplace book.

'Meanwhile, Inspector Knight has been questioning once again all those who work at the Egyptian Hall, regarding the death of Mr Tapper. He is starting with the performers who are due to move on to other venues. I cannot say that Mr Maskelyne is delighted with the arrangement, but he tolerates it.'

'Does Knight suspect anyone?' I asked.

'I rather think he may suspect young Mr Bromley. He is the only person who Tapper teased with the rope-tying trick. Bromley could easily have helped himself to the jute rope in the box office wastebin, to try him with it. Not with any ill intent; I am sure Tapper would not have seen him as a threat and would have submitted to being tied up by him. But the police will look at all possibilities. Was Bromley in the pay of

Ashbury? Ashbury might have considered him, thinking that Bromley would be in a position to learn Tapper's secrets. What might Mr Ashbury have promised young Bromley in return? Only he could say. Would Bromley have received anything? Of course not. In fact, according to the inspector, none of the possible suspects have shown any evidence of receiving unusual sums of money. This is not surprising since Ashbury was generous with his promises but little else.'

'Bromley said he had called into a chop house on his way home for some refreshment,' I said. 'Does that not give him an alibi?'

'I am afraid not. Inspector Knight questioned the manager and he was unable to say for certain that Bromley was there that night. The inspector has also commented that Mr Bromley might have hoped that if Tapper died, he would step into his shoes. I am sure that is not the case. I believe it would be most advisable if Mr Jennings was present at such an interview, and I will ask the inspector if we may also attend.'

We worked in silence for a while.

'Although I always welcome a mystery as an exercise for the brain,' commented Holmes, breaking the silence, 'it is occasionally a pleasure to solve one with little effort yet which brings great happiness to others.'

'I take it that you encountered one of the latter kind quite recently,' I said.

'Indeed, I did. I received a visit from Mr Barrett, the gentleman grocer of Bristol, with an earnest enquiry. It appears that my estimation of him was correct. When I spoke to him previously, I sensed that his liking for the Widow Winstone was rather stronger than simple friendship. He told me that he had been a widower for the last two years and was contemplating making her a proposal of marriage. He had been aware that there was something pressing on her mind, something she had not been able to speak of, but with the prospect of a closer relationship she told him all. It appears that after the death of her husband, some person wrote her letters suggesting that she might have been involved in the tragedy. She decided they were the work of a maniac and burnt them. The letters ceased, but then on the first anniversary of her husband's death she received another. This letter actually suggested that she had been in collusion with Tourmalin. She burnt that one, too. A letter in the same vein arrived each year. All, incidentally, were marked as having been posted in Bristol. She could not imagine who might dislike her enough to cause her such pain. Recently she received another, and having heard from Mr Barrett about my investigations, was considering whether she ought to consult me. A few days ago, she showed the letter to Mr Barrett, and he came to London and showed it to me.'

'She has no idea at all who might have sent it?'

'No, and neither did he.'

'Bristol is quite a large city,' I mused.

'It is. Fortunately, I had seen the handwriting before.'

'You had?'

'Yes. The notes taken on the day of the tragedy by Mr Brooks, the Bristol newspaper correspondent. He had no evidence to support his unfounded accusations against Mrs Winstone, but if Mrs Winstone had replied to them or made the letters public instead of burning them, he might have thought he had a sensational story to sell. Mr Barrett was overjoyed at my rapid solution to the mystery and has sent me a case of wine. I understand that wedding bells may chime very soon.'

We had paused for refreshment when there was a knock at the door and a note was delivered. 'It is from Inspector Knight,' said Holmes, tearing it open. 'Aha!' he exclaimed. 'I was right!'

'Oh?'

'He has heard from the authorities in Vienna, who have confirmed that a Herr Leonid Blumenthal, aged sixty-seven, died there in 1866 of pneumonia and was buried.'

'Was that as a result of the shooting?' I asked. 'Or did his earlier illness return?'

'Neither,' said Holmes. 'He died *two months* before Herr Blume was shot in Paris.'

'But —'

'Inspector Knight learned from the Parisian police force that Herr Blume was obliged to cancel his engagements in Vienna due to illness. Later, he appears to be well again, and an observer of the incident in Paris describes him as being in high spirits, using his magic wand as a ramrod to load the gun — an item wholly unsuitable for such a use. That man was not Blume, but Ashbury. Recall what Ashbury's father said of him. He admired Herr Blume; he wanted to *be* Blume. When Blume became ill and died in Vienna, Ashbury had the chance he had always wanted. He took over the act, the materials and the name. He had already been assisting Blume for almost three years and must have achieved some proficiency.'

'Could Ashbury have murdered Blume?' I asked. 'Is there a member of Blume's family who might have sought him out and taken their revenge? Was that why he was stabbed?'

'I don't think he was stabbed,' said Holmes.

'Oh,' I said. 'Well, how about the shooting in Paris? Was that real or a trick?'

'No, I believe Ashbury was shot, but not with a bullet,' said Holmes. 'A splinter must have broken from the wand which entered his lung. He was fortunate to survive, leaving a damaged lung and a scar. When he returned to his father, he accounted for his weakness in breathing by saying he had contracted pneumonia while abroad.'

'But he did not return to conjuring?'

'No, he decided to disappear. And with good reason. We were told that when he was in Paris, there had been complaints about Herr Blume regarding his behaviour towards young ladies. Nothing could be proved, but the police were watching him. That disgusting creature was not the real Herr Blume, who had never aroused any previous suspicion of bad character, but Ashbury, making use of his newfound fame. Remember what young Orlando Fishwick told us about Ashbury saying something objectionable to his sister, which resulted in her stamping on his foot? I admire such courage in one so young. It shows us that the beast cannot change his nature. Ashbury must have realised that it was only a matter of time before proof of his infamy emerged, and he was arrested. When he was injured, he decided to let it be thought that Herr Blume had died, his body taken to be buried in another city. When he recovered, he resumed his birth name and returned to England to live with his father. Herr Blume was no more. But Ashbury lived, and that was why he was murdered.'

Holmes quickly scribbled a note and went to arrange an urgent delivery to Inspector Knight. I waited for him, anxious for his return. 'What was in the note?' I asked.

'The identity of the killer of Alexander Ashbury,' he said.

CHAPTER TWENTY-EIGHT

'What?' I exclaimed. 'You know who shot him?'

'I have known for some time how the murder of Mr Ashbury was carried out and how the killer escaped,' said Holmes. 'The only question was the identity of the perpetrator. A number of persons would have been content with his demise, although only a few of them might have been capable of carrying it out. Also, the nature of the killing must be considered. It was a cold-blooded execution, done without hesitation. It has the quality of a personal vendetta, a revenge. The essential clues in the case are the missing overcoat from Ashbury's room, and the pattern in the dust on the clothing rail.'

'Oh,' I said, 'I don't think I noticed the dust. But the overcoat — has it been found?'

'I have told Inspector Knight where to find it, and also to examine the pockets.'

'What will he find there?'

'Residue from a recently fired gun.'

'Then the killer stole the overcoat that was on the rail?'

'No — the killer arrived *wearing* it. Recall that Constable Lewis saw it on the rail, but by the time we examined the room it had gone. There was, however, evidence that it had been there. An empty hanger on the rail and a pattern in the dust which showed that other items had been pushed aside just sufficiently to accommodate the coat.'

'The killer removed his coat and hung it up?'

'Yes.'

'Before shooting Ashbury?'

'No, afterwards.'

I must have appeared confused, because Holmes smiled at me.

'And the motive?'

'That is very clear. Consider the open shirt, the position of the second shot, the injury caused by a supposed stab wound, and the accusations levelled against the man calling himself Blume when he was performing in Paris.'

'It is a shame that the scar left by the shooting on stage could not be seen,' I said.

'That scar was obliterated by the murderer's second shot, the one which touched his skin,' said Holmes.

'A strange coincidence,' I said.

'It was quite deliberate,' said Holmes. 'The killer knew that Ashbury was the man who had impersonated Blume in Paris. Knew that he had committed unspeakable crimes. Would the wound in the chest of the dead man have led to this knowledge and thereby to the identity of the killer? It was unlikely, but possible. The killer did not wish to take that chance. The scar was destroyed by the second shot.'

'And then he escaped,' I said. 'But how?'

'Curiously enough, Stamford, it was your theory that the crime might have been committed by a trained monkey which set my thoughts on the right path,' said Holmes.

'He was shot by a monkey?' I gasped.

'No, but I considered who might have been able both to commit the crime and effect an escape. A person not only adept at firing a gun, but with a motive to do so, to protect a beloved sister from the clutches of a villain, and able, due to his small size, to escape by means of the slender branches of the tree.'

'Orlando Fishwick? Surely not! He is just a child.'

'He was a possibility, but I doubt that he could masquerade as an adult if he appeared at the door wearing a gentleman's overcoat. Also, an overcoat too large and heavy for him would not have been helpful in an escape. The same applies to his sister, and both working together. I dismissed that theory.'

'You say you know where the overcoat is?'

'Yes, it belongs to Monsieur Gaston.'

'Of course!' I exclaimed. 'He has a sister to protect. And he owns a gun.'

'Which leaves us with the question of how an adult wearing an overcoat escaped by means of the window. Would the branches of the tree have been able to hold such a weight without damage? I have examined them, and my conclusion is that they could not. I do not think the killer can have escaped that way.'

'Then how —? I don't understand.'

'It is simple, Stamford. You have all the facts.'

'But not your ability to put them together, Holmes.'

He took pity on me. 'The killer is Amelie Gaston.'

'No!'

'Mademoiselle Gaston and her brother were in Paris at the time Mr Ashbury was there, making the rounds of fashionable salons with his performances as Herr Blume. These included the leading hotels which were listed in the Paris newspapers. The list naturally included the Hotel Élégance, which was then managed by Monsieur Debrassie, their father. I would be very surprised if the manager did not allow his children, Armand and Amelie, to meet the distinguished visitor. I fear that Mademoiselle Gaston had an encounter with 'Blume' which so frightened her she told no-one about it. We know that other young ladies made complaints against him, and he was arrested and questioned, but nothing could be proven.

Only weeks later the accident happened at the Cirque Napoléon. If Mademoiselle Gaston had reason to avoid Herr Blume, she must have believed that she now had nothing to fear. Imagine then the shock she must have felt upon encountering him again recently at the Egyptian Hall, and realising that the man she had thought to be dead was still very much alive.'

'Do you think she told her brother?'

'Such an admission would have been more than she could bear. She had lived for several years in the belief that the man was dead. Now, she had to make it an actuality. Not only for herself, but for any past, present or future victims. Ashbury was drumming-up business, he had been handing out cards to performers with his London address. She sent him a note, which I suspect would have purported to come from her brother. He is a noted conjuror, and if he sought out Ashbury as a new manager, he would have been a valuable acquisition. But such a contract would have to be negotiated in secrecy. It was entirely understandable that the note requested that they should be alone and unobserved.'

'But Amelie was performing at the Egyptian Hall that night.'

'Only in the second part of the programme. Did she give an excuse for a brief absence? That is to be discovered. She wore her black mamba costume and borrowed her brother's overcoat and hat. She carried his gun in the coat pocket. She was admitted to the house by Ashbury. Once in the room, she revealed that she was Amelie Debrassie whom he had met twelve years before, in Paris.

Who knows what the conversation might have been? She must have led him to believe that she did not hold a grudge, and he admitted that he had personated Blume. She asked him to prove how he had survived the shooting, and he told her the

226

story of the accident — that he was shot not with a bullet but a fragment of wood. She asked to see the scar and he unbuttoned his shirt. That was proof enough. She shot him through the heart and as he lay dead or dying, she destroyed the scar and therefore her motive for the murder with a second shot.'

'And then she escaped? Without being seen?'

'Until that moment, Mademoiselle Gaston had been under the impression that there was no-one else in the house. She searched the body of Ashbury and retrieved the note, but then she heard the voices of Martha and her friend. Mr Robinson came upstairs and guarded the door while Martha ran to fetch a policeman.'

'She might have threatened to shoot Robinson.'

'She had no grudge against him, and there was always the risk he might overpower her. She opened the window and peered out, placing one foot on the frame. She saw the tree outside. But by now the earlier light rain had become a storm. Although in her costume she is capable of jumping to the tree, she was wearing her brother's overcoat, which she dared not leave behind. The upper branches were too slender to hold the combined weight and were slippery from the rain. Everywhere below was mud. She could not risk throwing the coat out and following it. She looked about for somewhere to hide. Behind the door — too uncertain. Under the bed — the space was cluttered with dusty boxes. She had one chance. She put the gun and her shoes in the pocket of the coat, removed it, and hung it up with the other clothes, which she had to move aside on the rail. She then removed the bedsheets from the box on which Osric stood, placed them either on the bed or on top of the other linens, and climbed into the box, folding her body to fit. She is slender as a snake, and the damage to the box had expanded it enough to accommodate her. There she lay, a dark shadow within. In that poorly lit room, the box must have appeared on a quick glance to be empty.'

I stared at Holmes, speechless.

'Constable Lewis certainly did not imagine that a human adult could be in the box. He sent Martha and Mr Robinson to wait in the kitchen while he went to make his report. The door had been broken open so it could not now be locked. Mademoiselle Gaston emerged from the box and restored the bedsheets to where they had been. She put on the shoes, coat and hat, and slipped down the stairs, unseen. In the hallway she took the umbrella to protect her from the storm. Now appearing as a youth, she may have secured a hansom to take her to Piccadilly. She was able to return to the Egyptian Hall in good time to perform her act. All she had to do was restore her shoes, coat, hat and gun to their usual places, and she was ready. She was in costume and is the one performer who has no need of greasepaint.'

'The umbrella?' I managed to say.

'To leave one's umbrella in a cab is not an unusual occurrence.'

'But —'

'Yes?'

'The inspector knew that Monsieur Gaston owned a gun. He said there was no sign it had been fired recently.'

'That is true. When Monsieur Gaston heard that Ashbury had been shot, he might have been concerned that his gun had been stolen. Imagine his relief when he found it safe — and his alarm when he saw signs that it had been fired. I expect he cleaned it well.'

'What will happen to Mademoiselle Gaston?' I asked.

'That is to be seen,' said Holmes. 'But if she is tried for the murder, it will be a very sensational case. I think leading counsel will be vying with each other to defend her.'

That was some comfort. 'So you now know the answer to the killings of Dr Peralta, Mr Winstone and Mr Ashbury,' I said. 'Only Mr Tapper's death remains a mystery.'

'Which is why I need to speak to Mr Bromley once more. But before I do so, I will request that Mr Jennings is present for that interview.'

The next morning, I met Holmes at the Egyptian Hall as it was about to open to the public. 'I have received a note from Inspector Knight,' he told me. 'Mademoiselle Gaston has confessed to the murder of Mr Ashbury and has been charged. Her brother is being questioned on suspicion of being an accessory but has not yet been charged.'

It was an outcome which saddened me, and I could only hope the courts would be merciful.

Mr Jennings was in the process of opening up the box office when we approached him. He looked unusually harassed. 'The police have been back here asking questions of everyone,' he said. 'I really don't know what else they can learn.'

'Have they interviewed your nephew yet?'

'No, they suddenly rushed away on another matter. But I am sure they will be back.'

'I would like to ask you some further questions on the subject of the jute rope used on the parcels delivered here. This type of rope is not normally held in the Egyptian Hall, and the only way it enters the hall is when it is used by suppliers to wrap packages.'

'That is true,' confirmed Jennings.

'I have studied some fibres swept from the floor in this building under the microscope and have found that they are of the same in composition as the rope used to tie Mr Tapper on the night he died — the rope which secured him so well, that he was unable to escape.'

Mr Jennings paled noticeably. 'It is a very common kind of rope,' he said. 'Anyone might have come here with a piece of it in his pocket.'

'Before I consider this unknown visitor, I must ask myself who here had access to that kind of rope, was present on the evening of Tapper's death, and had a motive to tie him so tightly that he was unable to make an escape,' said Holmes. 'Anyone to whom Tapper had boasted about his ability to escape being tied might have been tempted to test him. We also know that the late Mr Ashbury had a history of bribing persons to reveal the valuable secrets of magicians, so he could steal them and use them in his own business. Mr Tapper was undoubtedly in possession of such secrets and might have been subjected to some persuasion to reveal them. The new levitation apparatus which Mr Maskelyne had been working on was greatly envied by his rivals, and Tapper would have had a hand in the staging of it.'

'What of it?' said Jennings.

'I am giving you the opportunity, Mr Jennings, of being present when I next question your nephew.'

Jennings gasped. 'Mr Holmes, if you think that Peter had anything to do with this —'

'I think you can see why someone might suspect that.'

'Only those that do not know him,' Jennings protested. 'And Peter was not in the hall at the time. He was having his supper at the chop house. I know that because he told me he was going there. I gave him a shilling to spend.'

'A shilling,' said Holmes.

'Yes.'

There was a long silence.

'I think you will find that my nephew is a good, truthful young man, and more intelligent that he is often given credit for,' said Jennings. 'Many people do not understand him. If they suspect him, they might try to force him into a confession. I cannot allow that.'

'He mentioned having a shilling to spend on his supper that night, and I now know it was you who gave it to him,' said Holmes.

'Yes, what of it?'

'He left the hall earlier than usual because Mr Tapper told him he could. Maybe Tapper did so because he was expecting a visitor. Someone he could let in at the door unbeknown to Mr Maskelyne who was in his workshop. Was that visitor you, Mr Jennings?'

The expression on the manager's face told us that the question had struck home.

'You wanted to make sure your nephew was not in the hall when you called, so you told Tapper to send him away early, and gave him a shilling to buy his supper. That gave you enough time to speak to Tapper and return home before your nephew arrived. Yes, he is innocent. He had no idea that you had returned to the hall. All I need to know now is why you did what you did. Because I cannot imagine for a moment that you were Mr Ashbury's secret spy.'

Once Mr Jennings' initial shock had calmed, he looked almost relieved. He smiled. 'That is true. Ashbury had nothing to do with it.'

We waited. Jennings put up the closed notice on the box office and invited us in.

'I have told you the sad history of Peter's birth and upbringing. The cruelty and neglect of his own father. I recently discovered that that man is no longer alive; he burst a blood vessel in his brain during one of his rages and fell down dead. He left a small legacy for Peter which will mature on his majority. His future is secure. All I wish for now is his happiness and contentment. Mr Tapper threatened that. It seems he overheard some gossip in a public house, someone who had visited the hall and saw Peter sweeping the floor in the foyer and recognised him as a former inmate of the asylum. Tapper asked questions, was assured that it was true, and then he came to see me. He imagined that no-one would wish to employ Peter with his history and said he would tell Mr Maskelyne what he had found out unless I paid him for his silence. I laughed in his face. I told him Maskelyne knew everything and his attempt at extortion was a failure. In fact, I told him I would go to Mr Maskelyne and reveal what he had just said. I saw that this had frightened him. Which explains what happened next. He went on to make an implication about my relationship to Peter, insinuating that he was not my nephew, and placing a different, unfounded and wholly untrue interpretation. He asked me for money to ensure he would not spread that rumour. A large sum of money. I think I can guess where he imagined I might obtain such a sum. Of course, he knew that there are always those who prefer to believe the worst, even if it is a lie.

'I determined not to be blackmailed. I pretended to capitulate and agree to his terms. I said I needed to raise the money, and made an appointment to speak to Tapper alone, to discuss how I was to pay. Yes, I had secured some of the jute rope. I knew the fibres cling together in a manner very dissimilar to the manila. I made Tapper an offer, I said if he could free himself, I would pay him double what he demanded. If not, he must agree not to trouble me again and the whole matter would be dropped. He accepted the terms, but of course I had not shown him the rope I meant to use, and once he was seated in the cabinet and his back was turned, he could not see it. He himself directed me as to how Maskelyne and Cooke were usually tied. I followed his instructions. I threaded the rope through loosely at first, so he suspected nothing, and then I quickly pulled it tight and tied the knots. When he realised that he had been caught in a trick he was very upset. I told him that I intended to leave him like that overnight so that when he was found in the morning he would be shamed. He struggled to free himself so hard I thought the boards would break, but before that happened, he expired. I cut away the jute rope — which I took away with me — and replaced it with the manila. Then I let myself out of the hall and hired a hansom to take me home. I arrived before Peter. Naturally he is quite unaware of the events.'

Holmes nodded. 'I believe you,' he said.

'And now I shall go and speak to the police,' said Jennings. 'I hope they do not think I have confessed to something I did not do in order to protect Peter. They might charge me with manslaughter or even murder, but I may be able to convince them that it was an accident. There is one thing you can do for me.'

'Name it.'

'Please inform Mr Maskelyne that I have had to leave because of an emergency so he can ask someone to take my place in the box office.'

CHAPTER TWENTY-NINE

'So here is a strange thing,' said Inspector Knight when we next met with him. 'I received a visit yesterday from Mr Jennings who manages the box office at the Egyptian Hall. He told me that after speaking to you, he decided that his best course of action was to confess that he was the man who tied up Mr Tapper. What can you tell me about that?'

'Ah,' said Holmes, 'I am delighted that some resolution has been achieved. I did have a conversation with him yesterday in which I outlined the various possibilities in that case, and it appears that it gave him the resolve to do the right thing.'

'Well, it seems that Tapper's boasts were his downfall. Mr Jennings told me he determined to test his claims with a wager that Tapper could not extricate himself from a rope other than that used by Mr Maskelyne. Tapper agreed to take the wager and submitted willingly to being tied up. As we know, his heart failed him. Mr Jennings explains his next actions, substituting the manila rope, to make it look as if Tapper was alone, by saying that he feared if he simply reported this piece of foolishness, his employers would have less confidence in him. He has realised, however, that other persons were being suspected and great inconvenience was being experienced by further questioning, and that prompted him to reveal all.'

'I am not convinced that any offence has been committed,' said Holmes. 'What is the police view?'

'Our view is that we have more important things to spend our man-hours on, and we have accepted that Tapper's death was an accident. Mr Jennings has been given a reprimand for not speaking to us before and released without charge. I have told Mr Maskelyne that we are not making any further enquiries. What Mr Jennings chooses to tell him is his own business.'

'That must be a relief to all concerned,' said Holmes.

'I must thank you for the note you sent me on the Ashbury case, which has led to a substantial new investigation — the details of which my Chief Inspector tells me I am not yet in a position to reveal.'

'I hope Mr Fishwick has been exonerated,' said Holmes.

'He has, and two arrests have been made. The case should come before the police courts very soon.'

In the next week, Amelie Gaston and her brother appeared before a bench of magistrates. She was charged with the murder of Alexander Ashbury and he with acting as an accessory after the fact.

The examination of Monsieur Gaston's overcoat had, as Holmes had suspected, found a residue which showed that a recently fired gun had rested there. Gaston admitted having cleaned his gun, not because he thought it might have been used in the murder of Ashbury, but because he did not want unwarranted suspicion to fall on his sister. He had asked her if she had fired the gun recently, and she had told him she had borrowed it to practice shooting at targets. He had never known she might have had a motive to kill Ashbury. He was not aware that she had left the Egyptian Hall on the night of Ashbury's death. She had complained of a headache and told him she was retiring to the peace of one of the galleries to rest before her performance. She had returned in good time and in better spirits.

The charge against Monsieur Gaston was dropped and he was released.

Amelie Gaston made a statement to the police admitting her guilt in the killing of Ashbury, but said that she had arranged the meeting in order to confront him and get him to admit his crimes. She was afraid of him and took the gun to defend herself, but it had gone off by accident. She was leaning over him and on seeing that he was dead the shock had been so great that her hand shook, and the gun had fired a second time. She was sent for trial on a charge of murder, the prosecution making much of the accurate nature of the gunfire which it was claimed could not have been accidental. Amelie made an engaging figure in the dock, only occasionally raising her lovely blue eyes to gaze on the gentlemen of the jury. She was acquitted to enormous public acclaim.

Brother and sister enjoyed considerable fame thereafter and went on to a triumphant world tour.

Mr and Mrs Flowers and Mr Fishwick and his children formed a small travelling company under the auspices of their new promoter, Mr Archer, and were able to make a respectable living. Their comic sketch, 'The Foibles and Fancies of Osric', was especially popular, as was a spectacular illusion in which paper roses cascaded from a top hat to fill the entire stage.

Holmes, having persuaded Mr Fishwick that Tourmalin was no murderer, arranged a meeting between them, in which Mr Goodgold learned that he had been imprisoned in error, the explosion of the gun being due to a substitution of the ammunition by Dr Peralta on instructions of Ashbury. Since the perpetrators of the act were both deceased, and Goodgold had been convicted on his own confession of negligence, it was not possible for him to obtain any compensation. He was also most unwilling to air the business again, as he knew that he would never be able to shake off the reputation of having caused a man's death — some people preferring to believe the damaging and sensational over the truth.

In the following year, a novel entitled *A Romance of the Theatre* was published by a Mrs J. H., in which a beautiful songstress married a brilliant magician who was accused of making a fatal error with a rope trick. Donning the mantle of a detective she boldly determined to exonerate her husband, and braved numerous dangers and setbacks before she finally succeeded in unmasking the true culprit. It did rather well and was later adapted for the stage, with Mr and Mrs Goodgold taking the leading roles with great success.

Maskelyne and Cooke remained famed figures in the world of conjuring and illusion; their abilities to astonish and entertain can never be challenged.

Cabinets of many sizes and constructed from a variety of materials are still an important feature of the magician's performance. The true legacy of the fraudulent Davenport brothers, cabinets use darkness to conceal the truth, tell lies and deceive the eye. Some rely on the magician's skill, some use mirrors, false compartments, or black cloth. Some, like Mr Fishwick's, are not cabinets at all.

Holmes was unusually modest about his part in the Egyptian Hall case, but I could see that what was really engaging his mind was impatience to find another mystery which would test his skills. It was not long in coming.

HISTORICAL NOTES

Thomas William Tobin, to whose memory this book is dedicated, is an unsung hero of the art of illusion. Born in 1843, he was training as an architect by the age of fourteen. (His gravestone records a birth year of 1844, but his birth is registered in London, St Luke's district, in the first quarter of 1843. The 1861 census records him as an architect aged eighteen.) He later studied chemistry and was a researcher and lecturer at London's Royal Polytechnic Institution at the age of twenty.

Tobin was the inventor of a new kind of stage illusion using cabinets fitted with mirrors, requiring precise angles and sightlines. He patented the apparatus jointly with Professor John Henry Pepper, creator of the 'Pepper's Ghost' stage illusion, and demonstrated it in his lectures in April 1865.

The principle was soon adopted by stage magicians and must have been incorporated in Maskelyne and Cooke's early comic sketches. 'Will, the Witch and the Watch' was performed from 1871 to 1873 and was revived at the Egyptian Hall in 1881.

A modern performance can be seen here: **jimsteinmeyer.com/2023/10/31/what-we-hide-will-the-witch-and-the-watchman-from-the-stalls-part-two-2/**
Tobin died in America in 1883.

The popular saying 'every one must believe his own eyes' is declared to be a fallacy in *The Wonders of Optics* by F. Marion (translated from the French and edited by Charles W. Quin, New York, Charles Scribner's Sons, 1869).

Locations

The Egyptian Hall at 170 Piccadilly opened in 1812 as an exhibition and lecture hall. It was later refurbished as a theatre, and from 1873, under the management of William Morton, it became a dedicated theatre of magic, described as 'England's Home of Mystery'. It was demolished in 1905. Today its position is marked by the entrance to Egyptian House, 170–173 Piccadilly.

The space under the stage is known to have had a depth of only 40 inches. Performances took place in both the main hall and a smaller one, and there were exhibition galleries. Details of the internal arrangement of the stage and backstage described in this book are the author's own invention.

The Oak Leaf and the King Henry Tavern, which also appears in *Sherlock Holmes and the Ebony Idol*, are both fictional. The street where they are located is based on Maiden Lane. The Fallow Deer public house is also fictional.

Hoe Street Station has since been re-named Walthamstow Central. St Mary's Church is still a prominent feature of Walthamstow.

The first Waterloo Bridge was composed of granite and was opened in 1817. It was closed in 1934 and subsequently demolished. The current bridge was opened in 1942.

Characters

John Nevil Maskelyne (1839–1917). Born in Cheltenham, he was apprenticed to a watchmaker and became interested in the construction of mechanical devices associated with entertainment. When the Davenport brothers performed in

Cheltenham, he saw how the trick was done, and demonstrated that he could perform the same feats by conjuring. He and his friend George Cooke developed a career as magicians and came to London in 1873. They were lessees of the Egyptian Hall until 1904, before a move to the much larger St George's Hall in Regent Street. This was demolished in 1966.

On 10 October 1876 Maskelyne gave evidence at Bow Street magistrates' court in the prosecution of Henry Slade, who claimed to be a medium, and was charged with obtaining money by fraud. To the amusement of the court, Maskelyne demonstrated that Slade's spirit messages were the product of sleight of hand.

Psycho was originally exhibited in 1875. Retiring in November 1880 the mechanism underwent some modifications, before reappearing in 1884. Psycho is now held at the Museum of London and is brought out for special exhibitions:

www.davenportcollection.co.uk/wp-content/uploads/2017/06/Psycho-at-the-Museum-of-London.pdf

He can be seen in action (much modified from his early days) in an online video: **www.youtube.com/watch?v=0ZRvEwpN9UE**

Maskelyne often challenged the audience to discover how Psycho operated. The answer was detected early on, and an article published in January 1876 suggested the correct solution — compressed air. The article also describes in detail Maskelyne's presentation on stage. It can be found in *MacMillan's Magazine*, volume 33, pp. 241–7.

The original patent does not describe the precise manner in which the air pressure was manipulated, and it may have been modified over the years. It was sometimes suggested that Mr

Cooke was operating a bellows apparatus behind the scenes, and that is the method suggested in my novel for the performances in 1878.

Maskelyne's other less famous automatons were Zoe, Fanfare and Labial.

A short video constructed from photographs of Maskelyne plate spinning can be seen here: **www.youtube.com/watch?v=dLANRFlCR1U**

Mr Fishwick (Mr Fiz) and the claimed automaton Osric are inspired by the story of Boz and Yorick.

George Alfred Cooke was born c.1825–7 in Cheltenham. He married in 1872, but later left his wife to start a relationship with Fanny Fritz Bedwell. In 1878 he and Fanny were living in London where a son had been born to them in 1877. Following the death of his first wife in 1892, he and Fanny were married. He died in 1905.

William Campbell the Scottish Giant was born in Glasgow. Accounts of his age vary but he is often given the birth date of 2 April 1856. (*Newcastle Daily Chronicle*, 27 May 1878, p.3.) In 1878 he was landlord of the Duke of Wellington public house, Newcastle upon Tyne. The example of his humour in this book is from *The Era*, 17 March 1978, p.3.

Following his appearance at the Egyptian Hall he returned to Newcastle, where he was taken ill with congestion of the lungs. He also suffered from erysipelas. He died on 26 May 1878.

John Arthur Knight (1843–1883) rose to Chief Inspector Westminster B Division before his death at the age of forty.

Dr George Sexton (1825–1898) was a strong advocate of spiritualism and in 1873 delivered lectures critical of Maskelyne.

Ling Look, who was Hungarian, died while on tour in Hong Kong in 1877, but a younger brother adopted his name and took over the act. In 1881 he was performing in Brighton when the explosion of a miniature canon killed a member of the audience.

Edmund de Grisy. Accounts of this tragedy vary, but most consistently it is said that in 1826, de Grisy was performing 'the son of William Tell', in which he asked a spectator to fire a bullet at an apple in his son's mouth. A bullet would later be found embedded in the fruit. The bullets were made of wax, but a live round somehow found itself in the gun and the boy was killed. De Grisy served six months in prison.

Samuel Gilbert Scott, born c.1813, was an American daredevil and stunt performer, whose exploits inspired Mr Fishwick's foolhardy performance. Attempting a mock hanging on Waterloo Bridge in 1841, the rope slipped and Scott was dead when brought down. **https://en.wikipedia.org/wiki/Samuel_Gilbert_Scott**

In 1865, thirty-five-year-old Thomas Leatherbarrow tried to emulate the rope escapes of the Davenport brothers, and accidentally hanged himself. The inquest is reported in the *Sheffield Independent*, 20 May 1865, p.7.

Alexander Herrmann, known as Herrmann the Great (1844–1896), John Henry Anderson, known as the Wizard of the North (1814–1874) and Hartwig Seeman, known as Baron Seeman (1833–1886), were all noted magicians of the 1870s.

Charles Blondin (1824–1897) was the most celebrated tightrope walker of the nineteenth century. One of his many feats was to ride across a tightrope on a specially adapted velocipede.

Jean-Eugene Robert-Houdin (1805–1871). The legendary magician and illusionist inspired the art of modern conjuring, including amongst others, Harry Houdini. He was known to perform the bullet catch.

Other Notes
The mechanical chess-playing Turk was first exhibited in 1770 and destroyed by fire in 1854. It was later revealed to be a hoax, housing a human operator.

The bullet accident that happened to Herr Blume is inspired by the reported shooting of conjuror Dr Adam Salomon Epstein in Paris in 1869. Accounts of the incident vary; many state that he died from his injuries, others that it was a stunt performed to enable him to disappear as he was about to be arrested for gambling debts and sex crimes. It has also been claimed that the incident never happened, and the reports were falsified to drum up publicity. Press reports indicate that Epstein recovered and continued to perform, although his career appears to have declined due to gambling and according to Houdini (*see* TRAGIC MAGIC below) he died in miserable circumstances in Kiev.

Erysipelas is a bacterial skin infection which nowadays is treated with antibiotics.

The Council of India was established in 1858. Based in London, it was an advisory body to the Secretary of State for India. It was dissolved in 1935.

Holmes uses a pocket lantern in *The Sign of Four*, and *The Adventure of Wisteria Lodge*. Carriages were not provided with lighting until about 1885.

Principal Sources

The Era (1838–1939) was a weekly journal, which became known for its wide coverage of theatrical news

Hiding the Elephant: How Magicians Invented the Impossible by Jim Steinmeyer

Maskelyne and Cooke: Egyptian Hall, London 1873–1904 by George A. Jenness

White Magic: The Story of Maskelynes by Jasper Maskelyne

Lives of the Conjurers by Thomas Frost

TRAGIC MAGIC: A Survey of Fatal Conjuring, 1584–2007 by Joshua Jay

A NOTE TO THE READER

Reviews are so important to authors, and if you enjoyed this novel I would be grateful if you could spare a few minutes to post a review on **Amazon** and **Goodreads**. I love hearing from readers, and you can connect with me online, **on Facebook**, **Twitter**, and **Instagram**.

You can also stay up to date with all my news via **my website** and by signing up to **my newsletter**.

Linda Stratmann

2024

lindastratmann.com

Sapere Books is an exciting new publisher of brilliant fiction and popular history.

To find out more about our latest releases and our monthly bargain books visit our website:
saperebooks.com